OTHER

Harlequin Romances

by MARGERY HILTON

Many of these titles are available at your local bookseller, or through the Harlequin Reader Service.

For a free catalogue listing all available Harlequin Romances, send your name and address to:

HARLEQUIN READER SERVICE,
M.P.O. Box 707, Niagara Falls, N.Y. 14302
Canadian address: Stratford, Ontario, Canada.

or use order coupon at back of book.

THE HOUSE OF
THE AMULET

by

MARGERY HILTON

HARLEQUIN BOOKS   TORONTO
WINNIPEG

Original hard cover edition published in 1970
by Mills & Boon Limited, 17-19 Foley Street,
London W1A 1DR, England

© Margery Hilton 1970

Harlequin edition published April, 1972

SBN 373-01581-X

Printed in Canada

CHAPTER I

'I AM sorry, *mademoiselle*, I wish with all my heart that I could be of more assistance, but . . .'

Philippe St Clair's smile was rueful and his gesture eloquent as he looked at the young English girl who gazed at him so anxiously across the wide desk.

Melissa managed a smile, even though disappointment was heavy in her heart, and stood up, offering her hand to the courteous young Frenchman. 'You've been very kind, *monsieur*, and I've taken up far too much of your time, already.'

'But no!' Hastily he reassured her otherwise, a hint of regret mingling with admiration in a glance that at any other time would have assured Melissa that her fresh young charm lacked nothing to his Gallic eye. But at the moment her cornflower-blue eyes were shadowed with worry, the same worry that caused her soft curved mouth to droop in a way that was infinitely appealing, had she but known it.

Philippe frowned and checked his movement towards the door of the cool airy office that was situated in a quiet cul-de-sac in the business sector of Casablanca. He said, 'One moment—you have enquired at your Consulate, *mademoiselle*?'

'Yesterday—I've asked everywhere,' she said despairingly. 'I don't know where to start looking. My sister seems to have disappeared into thin air. I just can't understand it. She seemed to love her job here, and Casablanca, and—and everything. Why should she just throw it all over so suddenly and—and disappear? Without telling a soul where she was going? My mother's dreadfully worried. That's why I decided to come out and try to find her, before I start my new job and get tied up until I'm due for holidays again.'

She sighed. 'But you are busy, I mustn't interrupt any longer. Thank you for being so understanding, especially as my sister hasn't been very considerate in leaving you at such short notice.'

'It is of no consequence. *You* are not your sister. It is a pleasure . . .' He held open the door and bowed. 'But, please, if I can be of any assistance in any way while you are here, do not hesitate to contact me. Promise?'

She nodded, smiling her thanks again, and a moment or so later she emerged into the waves of heat-laden air that seemed more acutely marked after the coolness of the air-conditioning in the young *Directeur's* spacious office.

Impervious to the alien colour and bustle of the city, Melissa wandered along in the vague direction of her hotel. What now? And where? Oh, where was Avril? she wondered despairingly. Why hadn't she told them she was leaving her job, a job she'd pulled strings to land, playing blatantly on the indulgence of an old business colleague of their late father? The shadows veiled Melissa's eyes again. If only her father had been with them still; he would have known what to do, how to find Avril. He had been the only one who could ever make the wilful Avril see reason, who could command Avril's obedience. Certainly their mother couldn't, she was as ineffectual regarding her spoilt daughter as Melissa felt at that moment.

She opened her bag and took out the last two letters Avril had written home. The first one told her nothing, merely a little about the apartment Avril 'adored' and which Melissa had already located, only to find a stranger in residence who knew nothing of the former tenant, not even her name. There was a guarded reference to Philippe St Clair, whose charming features were still fresh in Melissa's memory, and a casual reference to someone called Sonia, who had a 'divine villa' at Rabat, and that was all. The rest of the scrappy letter consisted of a description of an Arabian silver snake bracelet she had bought in the *souk*.

It was the second letter which was so disturbing, and which had caused their mother to write two anxious letters, neither of which had succeeded in eliciting any reply, and finally Melissa's decision to fly out to Morocco.

Avril had written:

'Just a line to tell you not to write me at this address after the fifteenth as I'm moving. I've got the chance of a super new job, temporary, but it is still worth packing in my present one because for one thing the financial end is terrific and I'll be living lush with practically nothing to do, also I'll be travelling, and you know my wanderlust. Honestly, darlings, I'd be an idiot to turn it down. However, I can't give you an address to write to as I don't know myself where I'll be and when, so I thought I'd better let you know, and if you do want to be bothered writing it'll have to be c/o American Ex-

press for a week or two. Think of me lotus-eating—
love, Avril.'

Lotus-eating! thought Melissa despairingly. Not a
hint of what the wonderful job might be, where it
might be, and, more important, *with whom*! Mrs
Blair had been frantic, despite Melissa's own conviction that Avril was quite capable of taking care of her
worldly self and was well aware of all the pitfalls poor
Mrs Blair's fertile imagination could conjure forth.
Really, Avril was the limit! Why all the secrecy?

But why were her letters still lying uncollected in
their pigeonhole at the American Express? It wasn't
only exasperating; it was frightening.

Melissa returned to the name in the first letter.
Sonia. A villa in Rabat. It was so little to go on. If only
she knew the surname she might be able to trace the
unknown Sonia, perhaps find some indication of
Avril's plans, perhaps even some information which
would help her to trace Avril. But with only the first
name . . .

Melissa sighed, still not aware that her steps had led
in a totally different direction to that which she had
intended taking. The pensive veil cleared from her
gaze and a small exclamation escaped her as she took
in the narrow, sun-baked alley into which she had
wandered. A woman shrouded in a black hooded
djellaba, only her eyes visible above a thin dark veil,
watched her silently from a doorway, a white-robed
man in a red fez brushed past, giving her a curious
glance, and two emaciated dogs snarled over a scrap
of decaying refuse in the centre gutter.

Melissa quickened her step along the alley, conscious of the inky shadows lengthening and that she had no idea how far she had wandered. She reached the end of the alley, only to emerge into a street that was little wider than the one she'd just traversed, and looked uncertainly to left and right. She seemed to have landed in the native quarter. In the moments while she pondered turning back and trying to retrace her steps she heard the voices and saw the rush of urchins.

Instinctively she moved towards the gesticulating group a short distance along the street, and then a cry of horror sprang to her lips as she saw the cause of the incident.

The little street ended in a square on which converged the ends of two more dark little alleyways. From one of them had come a sadly overburdened donkey, to sink to its knees while the produce in the great panniers spilled and rolled in the dust. Three men gathered round, cursing the luckless animal, while the sticks rose and fell and the urchins crowded in to assist.

Melissa's white shady straw hat slid from her head and revealed the glowing titian tints which had evolved a certain tradition she had no hesitation in living up to as she rushed on the scene. Unheeding that her angry protests might not be intelligible, or that the consequences of her action might have unfortunate results, she waded in and seized the goad from the hand of the man in the dirty white *djellaba* and red *tarboosh*.

For a moment sheer surprise struck them silent and made them cease their belabouring of the poor brute. But it lasted only a moment before a torrent of Arabic

9

broke round her head. The urchins began to jabber and the man in the *tarboosh* raised his hands.

'Plis . . . Eengleesh lady! What you do? He is lazy beast. Stubborn. Eat too much!' He made expansive gestures around his own scraggy girth and grinned at his companions.

'That donkey's sick,' she cried, 'and half starved. How do you expect an animal to work if you don't look after it? Look!' She stared in horror at the pitifully thin flanks and the sores where the girth had frayed the dull coat raw over the ribs.

One of the urchins jostled close to her and thrust out a hand. 'Baksheesh,' he demanded impudently. 'English missy give baksheesh.' The others took up the jeering chant as Melissa tried to brush them aside.

She turned back to the men and said with a hint of desperation: 'That animal needs treatment. It's too sick to work, it——'

They were all talking at once, drowning her protests, and now their grinning expressions had altered. The man in the *tarboosh* made a grab at the stick she still held and wrested it from her hand. He said, 'You see, missy, he soon work again. We make him move.' From under grubby white folds he produced a box of matches and proceeded to mime the lighting of a fire, grinning and touching the stick as though it were hot.

For a moment she stared in amazement, then suddenly she understood and horror overwhelmed her. A dimly remembered anecdote returned . . . they heated a stone, or a charred stick, and applied it to the unfortunate animal . . . the practice had a name, she couldn't remember the term, and she found difficulty in believing that man could be so inhuman: now she knew—and believed.

'*No!*' she cried desperately. 'Listen, I—I'll pay for it to be treated. I'll find a vet—there must be one somewhere in—only don't dare——'

'English missy pay?' The man rolled his eyes. 'English missy mad. For that worthless, lazy spawn of a——'

'If it's worthless I'll buy the poor creature!' she cried wildly. 'How much is it worth? I'm not going to stand by and let you ill-treat it.' Her eyes flashing with an appearance of bravado and assurance she was far from feeling, she met the dark jeering gaze steadily. 'How much?'

The grins had faded now. The men and the urchins had closed round her in a circle and the dark faces were too close to her own for peace of mind.

'English missy has much money to buy very valuable animal? Worth many dirhans. How much will English missy pay?'

How much! What did a sick, miserable donkey cost on current market value? A small pathetic creature which at this moment looked as though it wasn't very far distant from whatever resting place a benign Allah may have set aside for man's beast of burden.

Melissa shook her head. She knew she had only about three or four pounds in dirhans with her at the moment. The rest of her somewhat limited funds was in travellers cheques at her hotel. She opened her bag, knowing as she did so how foolish was her action, as compassion and anger overrode cold common sense, and took out her purse.

Dark eyes watched avidly as she tried to reckon the still unfamiliar currency, then the man in the *tarboosh* waved his hand. 'English missy cannot pay. Not enough money. But this ...' A bony clawlike hand fastened round her wrist and fumbled with her watch.

Startled, she took a step back, trying to free herself, and the man grinned. 'Lady give watch. Take valuable animal. Lady get bargain.'

'No!' Suddenly frightened, Melissa struggled. She could not part with her gold bracelet watch, her father's last gift to her, but it seemed she did not have any choice. The jeering urchins gesticulated triumphantly as the gold glinted brightly in the man's hand and the circle of dark avid faces closed in on her again, intent on the purse she clutched tightly.

'English missy buy goods with donkey. We lose valuable animal. No sell our goods at market, and we very poor. Surely English missy have goodness of Allah in her heart and——'

Melissa looked round desperately, realising at last the predicament into which she'd walked so stupidly. They would 'persuade' her to part with everything of value she possessed and she hadn't a hope of escaping. She looked down at the hands importuning, sensed the determination that encircled her remorselessly, and gave a small cry as she tried to break out of the imprisoning group. Then her cry changed to a scream as she stepped on something and stumbled backwards, almost falling, and the hands scrabbled at her.

'No!' She tried to save herself and thrust them away, and then suddenly a sharp, imperious command cut into the gabbling voices and the dark clutching forms melted away.

A long shadow fell in front of her and a strong grip closed round her arm. The same imperious voice said sharply: 'Are you hurt? Have they robbed you?'

'I—I——' Melissa took a deep breath, swaying unsteadily, and brushed a tumbled tress of auburn from her flushed face. 'I—I—— They took my watch, but I——' She looked down, ascertaining that her purse was still clenched in her hand, then shook her head. 'No, but—— Have they gone?'

She took an urgent step forward, blinking at the now deserted square, empty except for herself and her rescuer, then the grip on her arm brought her to a standstill.

'One moment, young lady. You are surely not going in pursuit of that scum, or imagining that you will ever set eyes on them, or your watch, again? Or are you completely devoid of wits?'

'No! It wasn't like that at all.' Melissa came out of her daze and for the first time looked full into the face of the man whose commanding grasp still held her arm. What she saw checked the spate of indignant incoherencies trembling on her lips.

A dark compelling gaze burned down on her from the most arresting eyes she had ever encountered. They were so dark as to appear almost black at first glimpse, until one saw the topaz glints and the deep, tawny-hazel irises under the frames of heavy black lashes, and their sheer male arrogance was complemented by a severely chiselled mouth and a jawline of which the set betrayed both dominance and an inflexible will. His skin was smooth and dark, tanned to the hue of mahogany, and evoked in Melissa a mind-mirage of desert sands and wild winds under a blazing sun. Suddenly it came to her that his faultless English, the immaculate linen suit and the smooth assured

13

demeanour of him were but a mere veneer, disguising a ruthlessness she sensed instinctively despite her present moment of stress. This man would prove an unshakeable ally—or a remorseless enemy—if ever . . .

'I asked if you were hurt.'

'I——' She caught at herself, away from her strange thoughts. 'No, I'm all right. Thank you,' she added as an afterthought, then hurried on: 'You see, it was because of that donkey. It's sick, and I wanted to stop them ill-treating it, and . . .' Trying to phrase her explanation concisely, she turned as she spoke and knelt by the prostrate animal. Then an exclamation of distress broke from her and she looked up at the stranger. 'I—I think it's dead!'

The long shadow fell across her and he said in incredulous tones: 'You mean this is the reason for your foolish intervention which resulted in——'

'What else could I do?' she cried. 'I couldn't stand by and watch those brutes . . . do you know what they were going to do? They were going to . . .'

'You are English, of course,' he interrupted, a note of irony in his tone. 'Your concern over animals is notorious.'

'Not as notorious as some people's treatment of them!' she flashed. 'Oh, forget it. I must find somebody who will . . .'

'Do not distress yourself.' The touch on her shoulder was light but authoritative and the voice cool with command. 'It must also be true that the English sense of humour is strictly a private national business. Now, if you will permit me to take charge of this unfortunate affair, *I* will find the somebody.' The irony was evident now in his slight smile, and Melissa flushed.

14

He added, 'I would like to prove to you that we are not all barbarians and remind you that no country in the world is without those whose behaviour is not all we would wish.'

He moved from her and stooped over the donkey, his mouth compressing slightly then relaxing as he straightened. 'No, the animal is not dead, merely seizing this rare and unexpected opportunity to take a siesta.'

Unbelievingly she looked and saw that indeed he spoke the truth. The thin flanks heaved gently and regularly and as she watched one of the ears gave a slight flicker. Relief flowed through her and for the first time she smiled at her rescuer. 'Oh, I'm so glad. I thought the poor thing ... But what are we going to do? We can't leave it here. Do you know where ...?'

He gestured. 'Come with me and do not concern yourself.'

'But ...' She hesitated, seeing him move away with those arrogant strides, and then hurriedly followed. Surely he wasn't going to leave her now to deal with the matter as best she could on her own? But he had traversed only a few steps, to pause before an ornamental grilled gateway in the wall.

He opened it and waited, obviously expecting her to enter, and wonderingly she passed through to find herself in a cool courtyard where a pool shimmered in the rich afternoon sunlight and masses of white roses tumbled from a great ornate urn that stood in the centre. From the inky shadows within the Moorish colonnade of the house a white-robed figure came and hurried towards them. His thin bearded face was grave and scholarly as he greeted the stranger with a certain deference and bowed courteously to Melissa.

She wished she could understand the language as the stranger spoke quickly and the tall Moroccan led them indoors to a spacious room furnished with many cushions and silken hangings. Beginning to feel a little bemused, she seated herself on the broad bench seat that was placed down the length of one wall. A servant came almost instantly, and the Moroccan indicated the stranger, who spoke to the boy in crisp, fluent command. Meanwhile a second soft-footed boy had entered bearing a large chased brass tray which he placed on a low table in the centre of the room. The Moroccan busied himself at it, measuring tea from a small silver container into a tall, slender-necked teapot. A kettle was steaming gently on a little charcoal brazier and sprigs of fresh mint were laid in readiness on the tray. The delicate fragrance rose to Melissa's nostrils as her host gravely infused the brew, then proceeded to add several pieces of loaf sugar from another silver box which stood on the tray. Finally he poured the green liquid in small glasses and with a smile offered one to Melissa.

The stranger had come to sit near Melissa. He said softly, 'When you have sipped that you must accept at least two more glasses or you will break the custom.'

'It is most refreshing. I'm very thirsty.' She smiled at the tall Moroccan and said, 'You are very kind.'

'It is my pleasure, *mademoiselle*,' he said in English. 'You are enjoying your visit to our country?'

'Very much,' she said politely, delighted that she was able to converse in her own language.

He smiled. 'That is good. You must not allow those rascals you so unfortunately encountered to colour a

bad impression of your visit.' He took her glass to re-
fill it and brought a dish filled with almonds and small
plum-shaped sweets.

They proved to be delicious, but Melissa was becoming concerned about the passing of time. The
shadow of worry would not be subdued for very long
and there was also the matter of the donkey. She could
not leave it to its fate. She stole a glance at her watch,
only to realise that it was no longer on her wrist, and
could not repress a small murmur of dismay. The
Moroccan glanced enquiringly at her, but the stranger
had not missed that first small gesture towards the
slender wrist. He stood up.

'I'm afraid we cannot promise to restore your
property, but perhaps we can assure you regarding the
object for which you apparently bartered it. Come.'

Once again she was expected to follow this stranger
who seemed as at home within this domain as though
it were his own, and she found herself guided along a
stone-walled passage and into another courtyard, not
so ornate as the one she had first entered, and thence
through an archway into what was unmistakably a
stable. There, munching placidly at a heap of fodder,
stood the donkey. The panniers had been removed
and nearby a trough was filled with water.

'You see,' the stranger sounded mocking, 'he has
made a remarkable recovery.'

In the silence which followed she stared at the now
contented creature, aware that some comment seemed
expected of her but unsure of the form it should take.
She *should* be grateful, but there was something about
her rescuer that rubbed her the wrong way ... At last
she said doubtfully: 'Yes, but he's still dreadfully

emaciated, and there's that great sore on his ribs.'

'Agreed, but no doubt you will be planning to remedy that,' he said smoothly.

For a moment she did not respond, aware of that mocking humour in the dark eyes. His mouth tilted at the corners as he gestured towards the donkey. 'Well, wasn't that your motive in acquiring the creature? Tell me, what are you proposing to do next? Take him home with you to England? You will have to check up on how your quarantine laws apply to the importing of donkeys from Morocco.'

'But I can't . . .!' Dismay sharpened her expression and she gave a desperate gesture. 'I can't possibly take a donkey back to England! I wouldn't know what to—— Heavens, I never meant to—to actually buy the creature and—and—— I just didn't want him to suffer,' she ended hopelessly.

'Quixotic gestures have a habit of involving one to a greater extent than bargained for—as I suspect *I* am about to discover. But it is getting late. Come, I will take you back to your hotel.'

'Yes, but . . .'

He cut short her worried protest and gestured impatiently. 'For the moment the animal can remain here in Si Abrim's care, and we can discuss the matter on the journey.'

He turned away, and the arrogant assumption that she would meekly follow nettled Melissa. She said coldly: 'There is no need for you to inconvenience yourself any further. I can make my own way back to the hotel. As for the donkey, I realise it's my responsibility now and I'll think of some solution to the——'

He swung round so abruptly that she was quelled.

He said. 'You have been sufficiently foolish and impulsive for one day, have you not? Please endeavour to refrain from further irrationality. Or is it misplaced pride?' His glance flickered ironically over her set features. 'Are you so infernally proud that you scorn endeavours to help you?'

Phrased that way, his question precluded anything except a hasty denial, and he nodded slightly, appearing anything but mollified, and said coldly: 'Then let us take our leave of Si Abrim, before I begin heartily to wish that I'd left you to the mercy of those insolent jackals.'

Temporarily chastened by this scolding, Melissa took her farewell of the grave-faced Si Abrim and allowed herself to be escorted across the little square and through a bewildering maze of tiny streets to where an opulent white saloon was parked, almost blocking the narrow road. A dark-skinned chauffeur in immaculate white was waiting at the wheel, and he got out instantly, opening the rear door for Melissa as he responded to rapid directions from the stranger.

Melissa vaguely noticed a kind of crest on the car door, but there was no time for more than a blurred glimpse as she climbed into the luxurious pale blue leather interior. Her self-appointed guardian got in and closed the door, and Melissa was gratefully aware of the instant coolness within the car. It must be air-conditioning, she decided, glancing through the tinted glass of the windows and knowing a moment of idle speculation as to her whereabouts at the moment. They seemed to be travelling quite a distance, and the first doubtful little thought about whether the intended destination *was* her hotel had just occurred to her when her companion spoke for the first time since they had entered the car.

'You see,' he turned his head, 'you had strayed some considerable distance from your headquarters.'

The car was slowing at an intersection as he spoke and Melissa recognised the line of shops and the ornamental gardens a little farther along which fronted the hotel where she was staying. She felt a stir of guilty contrition for the moment of distrust and turned impulsively.

'I'm sorry, *monsieur*. I *hadn't* realised how far. Thank you for bringing me back, and—and rescuing me from those men.'

He raised one hand. 'It is nothing. Actually I am delighted to affirm something I have always felt to be true of English girls.'

'And what might that be?' she asked unwarily.

'That they are headstrong, wilful, erratic and impulsive—in everything but the matter of love.'

Melissa's head came up sharply. After a startled stare at him she said sharply: 'No, *monsieur*. If you are using my reactions as a yardstick by which to judge us you're going to be way out in your reckoning on the last point. For that is something you can't know.'

'No?' He got lithely out of the car and held out one strong, well-shaped hand to assist her. 'You sound very certain.'

'I am.' Melissa tried to appear cool and haughty and found it a difficult pose while blinking in the brilliance of the sun after the dimness of the car.

He was reaching back into the car for the hat she had forgotten and when he straightened he was smiling. 'Certain that I am mistaken in assuming English girls to be cool in love; or mistaken in my personal impressions of yourself?'

'Both,' she said firmly, refusing to be defeated, and saw the sardonic mouth twitch again. 'You should never judge by appearances—or hearsay, *monsieur*. Both can be very misleading. And now, goodbye and thank you.'

He inclined his head in a courteous salute as he took the stiff, formal little hand she offered. 'I quite agree, but how dull life would be if they were not.'

He stepped back a pace. 'And who knows, perhaps one day *Kismet* may prove us both wrong.'

It was not until some hours later that Melissa became aware of a certain omission in that afternoon interlude: that at no time had he given any indication of his identity. The thought did not seem of any importance, he had not offered his name, nor had it occurred to her to offer her own, and it was extremely unlikely that fate would cross two strangers' paths again.

Kismet . . .

How could Melissa know that *Kismet* had already taken a hand?

CHAPTER II

THE hours before dinner that evening seemed to drag
inordinately slowly. Melissa had showered and
changed, applied a leisurely make-up and groomed
herself to the final spray of cooling cologne, and found
that it was still barely seven. Too soon to go down to
the restaurant, even if she was hungry, which she
wasn't, and too late to go out anywhere unless she
made a night of it, which somehow didn't appeal, not
on her own.

She sighed, knowing she was only putting off the
task she was not looking forward to; that of writing
the letter her mother would be scanning every post for
after tomorrow.

She sorted out the packet of airmail paper she had
bought earlier that afternoon and sat down on the bed
to spell out her second day of failure.

Ten minutes later she was still staring at the blank
sheet and reflecting, not for the first time, on the un-
fairness of having a sister who had always been a law
unto her own wilful self and a mother who, dear as
she was, seemed to have no idea of the difficulties of
locating an elusive girl in a strange land.

'Of course you'll probably have to make a few enquiries, but I know you'll persist,' Mrs Blair had
declared, the evening before Melissa departed. Once it
had been decided that Melissa should make the journey her mother had veered to a mood of optimism.
The ghastly things one read about in newspapers

didn't happen to one's own daughter. It had probably been the fault of the post; Avril's letter had got lost—and she'd never been a terribly good letter-writer—or she might be in some place miles away from a post office. It could be a mix-up that was nobody's fault, but all the same . . . there was the possibility that Avril was ill and couldn't write, and she'd never have a wink of sleep until she knew for certain. After all, there was that time when Avril had been stranded in Greece, lost all her money, and the political situation so uncertain, and the Consul had had to advance her the fare home, and they didn't like having to do that sort of thing . . . and while lightning never struck twice in the same place, or so they said, Avril *might* be stuck in some dreadful plight somewhere . . . only the other week there'd been that business at the airport. They'd tried to kidnap that poor girl, and but for that American businessman's quick thinking they'd have got away with it . . . then they said it was all a joke . . . students, or something. No, Melissa must go, and be sure to write the minute she got there, and the minute she found Avril . . .

Melissa heaved another sigh and thought over her lack of success, seeking vainly for a note of hope she could express. But all that she could remember was a donkey, and a tall arrogant man who seemed to have a very poor opinion of English girls. What on earth was she going to do about that animal? She couldn't leave it with Si Abrim; despite his courteous hospitality he wouldn't want to be lumbered with a donkey. This was one worry she could have done without. But what else could she have done? And what about her precious wristwatch?

Melissa forced herself back to the task in hand and wrote: '*Dear Mum*,' and stopped again. Should she wait until tomorrow lunch time? Perhaps by then she might . . .

The bedside phone rang and she reached for it, frowning. They'd probably got the wrong room; no one here knew her. Unless by some miracle it was Avril . . .

But it was reception, to inform her that a Monsieur St Clair wished to see her.

Surprise gave way to a flare of wild hope. He'd heard something, remembered something, found . . .

He was waiting for her in the cocktail lounge. His attractive smile flashed, crinkling his eyes as they lit with appreciation of the picture she made in her jade nylon dress with its full, crystal-pleated sleeves and slender clinging lines. The appreciative glance took in the sleek shining coil of red-gold hair caught in a rhinestone band and then met her eager gaze.

'You look charming, *mademoiselle* . . .' His hand retained hers a fraction longer than necessary. 'I wonder, will you do me the honour of dining with me tonight?'

'Now . . .' She hesitated, and he said quickly: 'Forgive me, for thinking first of my own pleasure. You are hoping, of course, that I bring news of your missing sister.'

'Yes, I was.' She smiled. 'But, I'd like to dine with you, *monsieur*. I was feeling a bit . . .'

'Alone in a strange land? We must remedy that. But first, let us have an *aperitif*, and then I will tell you I have remembered something which may—I will not promise—be of help to you. But . . .' he shook his

24

head warningly, 'please try not to be disappointed. I should hate to be the bringer of a shadow to your eyes.'

He took her arm, then paused. 'You would prefer to dine elsewhere, perhaps? I have my car outside. Or shall we remain here?'

'Here, I think.'

He gave the charming inclination of his head that might have been practised—indeed, Melissa suspected that it was—but nevertheless this Gallic charm was both pleasant and easy to bask in, provided one kept two feet firmly on the ground! He escorted her to a table in a secluded, softly lit alcove and procured their drinks, then leaned forward confidingly.

'About a month ago your sister mentioned that she was going to spend a weekend with this American woman, this Sonia, at her villa. I doubt if she would have mentioned it if I had not invited her to drive out with me along the coast and she told me of this prior engagement.' Philippe paused, his dark eyes rueful. 'How I wish I had queried further, that I could tell you the name of this Sonia. But your sister was rather a mysterious girl. She would not accept my invitations to show her something of the fascinating haunts of this country. She used to smile and say she did not believe in forming personal relationships with her boss, and look at me with that prim little English-girl look of hers.'

Melissa suppressed a wry smile; she knew Avril's 'mysterious' act very well, and also that Avril was very well aware of its calculated effect on men. Avril must have found someone extremely attractive to have been diverted from a conquest of Philippe St Clair. However, she made no comment except to nod and waited for him to continue.

'Naturally, I could not persist, but when she returned on the Monday I asked her if she had had an enjoyable weekend, and she announced that she had been caught trespassing. When I asked her what she meant, and jokingly asked her if I would have to come and bail her out, she giggled and said it wasn't like that at all. She looked extremely—how do you say it? —extremely smug and said she had met a mystery man and fallen under his spell. That if it hadn't been for Sonia she was sure he would have captured her and held her prisoner in the house of the amulet.'

'Prisoner? In the house of the . . .?' Melissa turned pale. 'Where was this? And who was this man?'

'I'm afraid I can't tell you,' he said sympathetically. 'I wish I could. I asked her; what was this prison like, with the amulets, and she said it was a most beautiful house with a fairy-tale garden, with almond trees and an aviary of singing chaffinches, but over every entrance there was an amulet, one of those horseshoe things. She laughed then and said she was looking forward to her next visit to Sonia's villa. She didn't refer to the matter again, but I could tell she was intrigued and weaving some imaginary tale round this house. Then a couple of weeks later she told me she was leaving, and the rest you know.'

Melissa didn't know what to make of it. Avril could be feather-brained at times, but her fantasies did *not* usually revolve round fairy-tale gardens and almond blossom—or strange houses guarded by talismans.

Philippe broke into her reverie and asked if she would like to go in to dinner. Over it, reflecting that she mustn't be too doleful a companion, she tried to divorce the matter of Avril from her thoughts and let the conversation drift into a lighter sociable vein. For a moment she was tempted to recount the incident of the afternoon, then changed her mind; somehow it was a story from which she did not emerge very brightly, she decided ruefully, afraid of evoking Philippe's amusement.

They had reached the coffee stage when Philippe said suddenly: 'You are still deeply worried, are you not? And more so since I told you of this house and Avril's man of mystery.'

'Yes.' She sighed and the mask of assumed gaiety fell from her, leaving a vulnerable, secretly frightened young girl.

'I have been thinking,' he reached across the table and touched her hand. 'It should not be too difficult to locate this mysterious house of the amulets. We know that the villa lies just outside Rabat, on the coast, and I think that the house can not be so far away if Avril walked there. I'll admit that we may be looking for a needle in a haystack, as you would say, but I know the area quite well and I think it is worth while making the effort.'

'I—I'd give anything to find her, but it seems a great deal to expect. I mean,' she shook her head, 'it would take so much of your time and you have your business ... It's very kind of you, but I don't want to impose.'

'It would be a pleasure, if you would let me help in your search,' he said quickly. 'After all, to some extent I am responsible. Oh yes,' he interjected as she started to protest, 'I should have made sure where, and with whom, your sister was going. Instead,' he shrugged with charming shame, 'I allowed pique to claim me because a cool little English miss showed herself completely proof against me. So this way I can make amends, if only you will permit me.'

'Well, if you are sure . . .' she said doubtfully, 'but I could hire a car and try myself if . . .'

'No, you must not,' he said with an expression of horror. 'Supposing that you also vanished! *Mon Dieu!* No, I insist. But it is a long drive. We must start off very early, so that we have plenty of time to search. And now,' he smiled, 'that is agreed? Then shall we dance . . .?'

It had been a delightful evening, even more delightful for being unexpected, and Philippe the most charming and attentive escort a girl could wish for, thought Melissa very early the following morning as she lay in bed and sipped her morning tea. How different he was from the autocratic stranger she had encountered the previous afternoon. And yet . . . Melissa frowned into space. His arrogant hawklike features had an annoying way of leaping back into her mind's eye, as though that compelling power could still reach round her from time and space. But why, goodness only knew. He certainly hadn't endeared himself to her. He was neither charming, gentle nor sympathetic, on the contrary, he . . .

Melissa pushed the thought away and contemplated the day ahead, aware of a lightening of her spirits as she thought of Philippe St Clair. What a difference it made when there was someone with understanding to share problems.

Philippe arrived promptly in a sleek, powerful

Mercedes convertible. Following his advice she had donned a filmy white headscarf and enormous amber-framed sunglasses, and once they were clear of the city she realised the reason for his advice. Philippe believed in speed, and soon the wind was whipping the flying ends of her scarf and trying to tease out every unguarded tendril of hair.

He had chosen to take the coast road and in a very short time they passed Mohammedia and the road was winding along near the sea. Melissa said wistfully: 'How tempting it looks. Do you know, I haven't been in the water yet.'

'I'm afraid you are going to be unlucky today,' Philippe told her. 'If we once set foot on one of those beaches I can assure you we will not discover our mysterious house today.' However, he did stop long enough for them to partake of tiny cups of sweet black coffee and sugary almond croissants which left their tell-tale feathery flakes round Melissa's mouth and evoked a great deal of teasing amusement from Philippe. She was laughing when they got into the car and resumed the journey, and the warm lights were glowing in Philippe's dark eyes. But they had sobered by the time they neared the capital and Melissa began to wonder dazedly where they were to begin their search for a house they knew neither the name of nor where it was situated. However, Philippe looked a great deal more confident than she felt, and over lunch he propounded his theory.

'The way I see it,' he said thoughtfully, 'we won't have to go too far from the city. When Americans take a villa they want every civilised amenity, their ice and comfort. They like their water sports and sophisticated amusements, so we will try the most popular *plages* first, and we will enquire among the locals about a house such as your sister described. But again,' he pursed his mouth wryly, 'you must not hope too much. You must remember that Moorish decoration frequently included symbols which your sister might have described as amulets. It is the aviary of birds on which I am pinning my hopes.'

All during that long, sun-baked afternoon Melissa tried to maintain an air of confidence, but as the hours and miles passed she could not ward off bemusement. Palm-fringed boulevards, dazzling beaches, white villas, Spanish villas, plain and stark, elaborate and landscaped, sun-bleached stone and pink-washed brick, cars, tourists, donkeys, sun-varnished bodies and boats and beach umbrellas, and another turning on a road that went on for ever, and another vista of more white villas and . . .

'Oh, Philippe, you must be exhausted,' she said when they flopped back into the car and stared at the deepening haze in the west. 'Please turn back. There's that long drive back and you must be tired.'

'Driving does not bother me,' he smiled, 'not when I have so charming a companion.'

'You're very kind, but you mustn't worry any more. I'll have to . . .'

'You have to do nothing. I do not like being defeated and this was my suggestion. But I do know one thing,' he said with a sigh, 'I cannot face one more café table and mint tea! Now, I wonder . . .' He reached again for the map and spread it across his knees, tracing their routes with the tip of a slim silver pencil.

She sat silent, not for the first time secretly cursing the thoughtless Avril, and then rebuking herself. If anything *had* happened to her sister she would never forgive herself for the impatient condemnation. Philippe gave a murmur, raised his brows at her enquiring glance, and briskly folded the map. He switched on the engine again and said briefly: 'One last detour. Maybe this will prove our goal. Put your faith in *Kismet, mon ami* . . .'

He took a minor turning a little farther on and drove more slowly, scanning the open countryside and frowning slightly. Presently the road dipped through a shady grove of palms and opened out as the trees thinned and the beginning of a village straggled into view. The sea came into sight as the road topped a rise and there was an untidy rash of partly built chalets strewing the long shallow incline down to a wide deserted bay.

'They are opening out—developing a new tourist centre here,' Philippe explained, 'and I believe there are a few villas farther on which were built solely for letting to wealthy visitors.'

'They're spoiling all the beautiful places now with this endless tearing up and building hotels and flats that haven't a scrap of character about them,' she said sadly. 'It seems a shame.'

'The march of progress,' he responded flatly. 'And it does bring a measure of prosperity that is often sorely needed. Ah, we will ask this old lady and pray that she understands my *patois*.'

He slowed to a halt as they overtook an elderly woman wending her way home and carrying an enormous basket of provisions on one arm as she hauled a sleepy-eyed child along in her wake.

The child promptly forgot its sleepiness and came to stare at the car and Melissa. She smiled at it and shook her head at the question she couldn't understand, then recalled that she should still have a few fruit drops in a packet in her bag and sorted them out. The language of sweets was universal, she thought, watching the small cheek bulge and the owner turn its attention to the colourful array of badges adorning the front of the Mercedes. But Philippe didn't seem to be having much more success this time than on all the foregoing times Melissa had now lost count of. He seemed to be having difficulty in making the old woman understand, and Melissa experienced a fresh sense of futility. Even if they did trace either the villa where the American Sonia stayed or the house with the amulets there was little hope of it leading to Avril. The American woman had probably left ages ago, after all, several weeks had elapsed, and it was unlikely that she would stay for a great length of time, unless she had friends or business interests to keep her there, and as for the mysterious house and its owner; well, Avril had admitted to trespassing. What proof did they have that she'd ever gone back...? Then she saw Philippe turning back towards the car with an expression of triumph lighting his face. Melissa took a deep breath and found she was holding it as he jumped lithely into the driving seat.

'Have you...?'

'I think we have—at last!' he grinned. 'There was a party of Americans staying here in one of the new villas—but they left only a couple of weeks ago, unfortunately, and our amulet house is a couple of kilometres farther down this road.'

'I don't believe it,' breathed Melissa.

'You will very soon—though the party of Americans may not have been Sonia's crowd.'

'Did the old lady know anything about the owner of the amulet house?'

Philippe frowned. 'I am still trying to sort that out. Her French was very limited and my Arabic is anything but fluent, but I gathered that this house was owned by the old Amghar of Kadir—Kadi el Kebir—wherever that is—and now belongs to the young Amghar of Kadir, but he is rarely seen there, and the *tigemmi* has received the young *lalla* from across the *aguedal,* whom the new Kadi el Kebir is expected to take as his bride because the old Amghar——'

'Start again,' said Melissa. 'Slowly.'

'This house seems to be part of an estate belonging to an old French–Moroccan family, but don't ask me where the rest of it is, and whoever he is he seems to be held in some esteem, apparently known as the great lord or judge, past tense, because a new Amghar means the old boy has passed on. Anyway, it's a start, so let's go, *mademoiselle*!'

'Did you ask about the aviary of singing birds?' Melissa asked.

'I did. This was what brought the first sign of recognition, then the family history began,' Philippe grinned. 'There was a great deal more, if I'd been able to follow it more clearly.'

'Yes,' said Melissa, her mind already running along another line of thought. 'If nobody is living there who is looking after those poor little birds?'

'Oh, *mon ami*!' Philippe slowed to take a sharp

bend in the track. 'Let us worry about your sister first.'

'Yes, I know, but surely no one would leave all those birds caged without food and water. Not in this heat. They'd die.'

'What a tender-hearted little creature you are.' Philippe braked and turned to look at her, his expression amused. 'Do you save all that tenderness for *birds*?'

She smiled ruefully. 'Maybe it seems silly to you, but I can't help feeling this way for creatures who suffer because human beings don't care.' She hesitated, colouring a little under a dark stare that had become rather intent. 'Are we there?' she asked, looking at the wild spiky scrub bordering the track.

'Not quite.' Philippe's dark gaze did not waver. 'I was reflecting on how totally different you are from your sister. Forgive me, it is I who digress from our purpose.'

The car rolled forward again and a few minutes later passed into the inky shadows of a high wall that was flush with the edge of the road. Outside a narrow grilled gate Philippe drew to a halt and gestured. 'I think this is our destination. Shall I investigate first?'

'No—I'm coming with you. Look!' She pointed at the curved shape let into the grille. 'Is that the amulet?' She sprang out of the car and went to examine it more closely, shading her eyes against the brilliant lattice of sunlight pouring through the gate.

It was more of a wishbone shape than a horseshoe. An inverted half moon crossed the lower point of the curve, two little star-shaped pieces tipped the points of the crescent and two curved bars crossed the arc of the shoe itself. Melissa's eyes narrowed. She was certain that she'd never seen this particular talisman before, yet somehow it seemed familiar. She thrust at the gate, then turned to Philippe. 'It's locked.'

'There will be another one,' he said calmly. 'Come, we will find it.'

Sure enough, farther along, round the angle of the wall, they came to another more imposing entrance. This was wider, wide enough to permit the passage of a car, and it swung open to the touch. Wonderingly, after a glance at the amulet, she passed through and looked at the long, beautifully tended garden within.

There were the almond trees, the pools with their tiled surrounds and lotus blossoms glistening under the soft spray of the fountains, and somewhere unseen singing birds trilled and chirruped. The path wound under a series of pergolas and opened on to a paved courtyard fronting the house. Above the Moorish colonnade was a long balcony of intricately wrought iron and below was a massive door of studded bronze. On the door hung the amulet, and over the house and garden there brooded a silence that made Melissa draw nearer to Philippe without realising that she did so.

She stared up at the amulet, and the heavy ring beneath it, and listened to the dull sonorous echoes as Philippe plied the ring against its base.

She did not really believe that there would be any response, until a soft clicking noise drew her attention to the small grille at eye level and the panel that had slid away behind it. Light gleamed on the eye that stared into her own, and with a small exclamation she drew back. Philippe's hand steadied on her arm, and

35

the door swung slowly open.

An impassive-faced manservant stood there. His eyes dark and suspicious in his swarthy, heavy-jowled features, he made no sign of enquiry or greeting, merely waited for them to speak.

After a glance at Melissa the young Frenchman said courteously: 'May we speak with your master? We wish his aid.'

'My master is not at home, *monsieur*,' the man said in a thick, heavily accented voice. 'What is your business with El Amghar?'

Philippe hesitated. 'We have come a long way. We had hoped . . .'

'Perhaps I may be able to assist Monsieur. You are tourists, in difficulties, perhaps?'

'No.' Melissa took a deep breath. 'We are looking for someone. My sister. I believe she came here some little while ago. She told us she———'

'A young English lady?'

'Oh yes!' Melissa's face lit up hopefully. 'She described this house and the Amghar—at least I think it must have been the Amghar—and we wondered if . . . You see, we've lost touch with her and it's terribly important that we find her. Have you any idea where she went? If she went with the American lady called Sonia. You see———'

Philippe's grasp tightened on her arm and silenced her. He said, 'We know Miss Avril Blair came here. And we feel sure your master will remember her and be able to help us to find out what happened to her.'

'I am sorry, *monsieur*,' the man was stepping back, 'I know no one of that name.'

'Yes, but . . . are you sure?' Philippe said urgently.

'She did come here several weeks ago.'

The door was beginning to close. 'There has been no young English lady of that name here, *monsieur*.'

'But maybe you did not see her,' said Melissa desperately.

'I have been here all the time. I assure you, *mademoiselle*, there has been no English lady here, ever. You must be mistaken. I am sorry, I cannot help you, and neither can my master. *Bonjour, mademoiselle . . . monsieur*.'

The door closed, leaving Philippe staring at it, and Melissa with all the colour drained from her face.

*　　　*　　　*

'I think . . . perhaps I did make a mistake. That cannot have been the house of which Avril spoke.'

'I'm positive it was,' said Melissa. 'I just have an instinct that we were on the right track, and what's more I didn't believe that manservant when he said he'd never seen Avril. There was something about his expression . . .' She sighed. 'Oh, I don't know . . .'

They had finished a very late dinner after their long drive back from Rabat and were sitting in a secluded corner of the lounge in Melissa's hotel. Philippe nursed a drink, and his dark brows were drawn into a worried frown. 'I am almost inclined to agree with you,' he said slowly, 'except . . . it is quite possible that he did not see Avril, even if she was there that day.'

Melissa could see the truth of this, yet some instinct persisted that Avril had returned to that house of the singing birds and the strange amulets. She said in a troubled voice: 'What are we going to do next? She must be somewhere. But where?'

'Morocco is a large country in which to search,' Philippe said gently. 'I think now you should rest. You must be weary, *mon ami*, you are not yet used to all this sun.'

She smiled faintly. She did feel utterly weary, almost lightheaded. 'I can never thank you enough for your help, Philippe,' she said impulsively.

'It is nothing.' He shook his head. 'If I may, I will call you tomorrow. Perhaps a new day may bring new hope.' He rose with her and walked with her towards the lift. '*Bonne nuit*—try to forget to worry for a little while.'

He took her hand and raised it to his lips, then stood back, giving a small inclination of his head as the lift doors opened and she stepped inside.

She felt strangely alone and bereft as she was borne up to her floor. Back in her room the first thing she saw was the letter she had left unfinished the previous evening. Her heart felt leaden again; how was she going to break the news to her mother that all her efforts to trace Avril had ended at blank walls? If it hadn't been for Philippe ...

She began to make preparations to retire and she was on the point of switching off the bedside lamp when a thought occurred; she had not enquired at the desk when she returned with Philippe. There might have been a message for her from one of the many sources where she had made enquiries. She hesitated. It was a slender hope, but she might as well ring down and have it quenched ...

The day clerk had gone off and the voice that responded sounded vague, with its 'One moment, *made-*

moiselle . . .' There was a long wait that seemed interminable, and she was on the point of giving up when the voice came, more sure now. 'Yes, there was a message earlier this evening . . . Mademoiselle did not receive it . . .?'

'No.' She was breathless.

'The name was Blair, *mademoiselle*. A gentleman on behalf of Miss Avril Blair. She wishes you to go to her immediately, and a car will be sent for you tomorrow at eight-o-hours. That was the message, *mademoiselle*. Do you wish a copy?'

'No, thank you—thank you very much.' She put the receiver down and experienced a wave of relief that made her feel weak. Avril was safe! Thank heaven; Avril was all right.

She stared at the telephone, tempted to ring down again and ask for the written copy, if only to convince herself that she hadn't imagined it. Of course she hadn't imagined it; tomorrow she would see Avril, and wouldn't she give that young lady a piece of her mind for all the worry she had caused, to say nothing of an enforced—and expensive—holiday Melissa had not intended to take.

It was not until she was lying in the darkness that the questions began to loom. Why hadn't Avril phoned in person? Why hadn't she come herself if she . . .? How had she known Melissa was here?

Morning light did not bring the answers, only a fresh wave of uncertainties.

Melissa gave up attempts to finish her breakfast and wondered if the message constituted an invitation. Avril said to join her. But where? How far away? And with whom? She drank some coffee and checked the time, still caught out every so often by the lack of her wristwatch, and returned to her room. The hotel was hardly astir at this early hour and the only other occupants of the dining room had been a couple who were leaving that morning.

Trying to assure herself that in a very short time she would be seeing Avril and the mystery would be cleared up, she put on a fine film of make-up, collected her sunglasses and a light jacket in case she needed it, and went down to wander restlessly around the hotel foyer.

At exactly one minute to eight a middle-aged man in immaculate European dress entered the lobby and crossed to the desk. The clerk leaned forward, then indicated Melissa and the man came across the black and white mosaic with curiously soundless footsteps. In very good English he said: 'Miss Melissa Blair?' and when she nodded, said courteously, 'The car is waiting, *mademoiselle*, when you are ready.'

She hesitated. 'But isn't she—isn't Avril here? I thought...' Unease was back in full force now and she stared at the man, searching the rather full, fleshy features and dark eyes for an indication of character she could trust. He didn't look in the least sinister, if anything he looked rather tired and worried. He returned her scrutiny quite calmly, and she said: 'What's your name?'

'Mahmoud,' he said quietly. 'I am to drive you to join your sister, *mademoiselle*.'

'Yes, but ... I thought she would be coming to meet me herself.' Melissa bit her lip. 'Is Avril all right? She's not ill, or anything?' she asked anxiously.

'Please do not be alarmed, *mademoiselle*. Your sis-

40

ter is in excellent health and looking forward to being reunited with you.'

'But couldn't she come herself?' A feeling of desperation made Melissa look round helplessly. 'Why didn't she let me know sooner?'

Mahmoud began to betray the first signs of impatience. 'I can't tell you, *mademoiselle*. I am merely acting on instructions. That I was to bring the car here and drive you to the house where your sister is a guest of Miss Amorel Vayle.'

Still Melissa hesitated, torn by suspicion and indecision. The name didn't mean a thing to her, but then why should it? Oh, if only she could be sure she wasn't walking into a trap. But why should it be a trap? Avril had left her job of her own free will. She hadn't suddenly been spirited away. She had written quite calmly to say she had found something new and lucrative. And who else but Avril could have been responsible for the message and the arrival of Mahmoud? Then she saw Mahmoud take a pace back.

He said, 'Mademoiselle does not wish to comply.' With a brief salutation he turned briskly away.

She saw the doors swing behind him and his portly form cross the lobby and disappear from sight, Melissa came to life and rushed across the foyer. She emerged outside into the fresh sweetness of the young day in time to see Mahmoud getting into a light blue saloon with an open sunshine roof. She shouted, and he leaned across to open the passenger door.

He smiled at her. 'Mademoiselle has decided not to disappoint her sister, after all. Would you prefer to sit in the rear?'

'No, this will do.' Vaguely noting that the car was

41

quite empty apart from Mahmoud and wondering why she had expected anyone else, she climbed in and sank back breathlessly.

He must have started the engine immediately he got in, for the car slid forward the moment she closed the door. So obviously he had no intention of kidnapping her, she thought wildly, when he was prepared to depart without her.

After a moment or so he said: 'There are cigarettes under the dash, if Mademoiselle wishes to smoke.'

'No, I don't at the moment, thank you,' then, 'Is it very far away?'

'Quite a long way, *mademoiselle*, which is why we travel early.'

'Before it gets so hot.' Remembering Philippe giving the same reason she could understand that. She would have to let him know later on, he wouldn't be at the office yet . . . The morning bustle was beginning in the business quarter and she sensed an impatience in Mahmoud to be free of the city's confines and knew she had not been mistaken when they reached the outskirts and the car responded to increased pressure on the throttle.

She looked at the highway stretching ahead and noticed another kilometre stone marker flash by with its sign saying P7. Wasn't that the Marrakech road?

Presently she said: 'Are we heading for Marrakech?'

'Mademoiselle is observant.' Mahmoud's concentration did not slacken for an instant. 'Yes, we should be there before lunch.'

'It's farther away than I expected,' she said uneasily.

'Is it?' he said calmly. 'I'm afraid we have to go a little farther beyond Marrakech, *mademoiselle.*'

He lapsed back into silence and Melissa tried to quell her unease and watch the passing scene. At least she was seeing something of the countryside! The drive yesterday with Philippe, and now Marrakech . . .

After a while Mahmoud asked if she was quite comfortable and if she would like to stop for coffee. She shook her head, telling him she would prefer to reach journey's end and her sister as quickly as possible. Mahmoud nodded and the car increased speed, then he added: 'There is a hamper with flasks of wine and coffee on the seat behind you, *mademoiselle*, if you should feel thirsty. It is perhaps hotter than you are used to.'

He seemed solicitous enough for her comfort, she thought, relaxing slightly, and really, she had gone off perfectly happily with Philippe yesterday and she knew little more of him than this new stranger who had entered the scheme of things.

They stopped for lunch at a small, fort-like hotel some fifteen kilometres south of Marrakech. Again she sensed Mahmoud's impatience to be back on the road, even though he insisted that she refresh herself and walk round the cool *ryad* where the fountains played and time seemed to reach back to an ageless peace. But the brief sense of peace fled when she finally realised where they were bound.

All across the great plain they had traversed the mountains had dominated the horizon; the blue-misted peaks of the High Atlas.

Dismay numbed Melissa and blinded her to the cool green slopes and the wild beautiful valley up

43

which the road zig-zagged into a vista of Alpine grandeur. A fast-running stream sparkled blue among the rock crevices and was lost as another bend revealed a glimpse of the panorama left behind before it curved and was lost to view. The purple shadows were beginning to lengthen and panic seized Melissa. She turned fiercely to Mahmoud.

'Why didn't you tell me it was all this way? Where are we going? I—I don't believe you're taking me to Avril! But why? *Why?*'

'But you would never have consented to accompany me if I had told you of this long journey,' he said in expressionless tones. 'And I assure you, at the end of this wearisome journey you will be reunited with your sister.'

'I don't believe you,' she cried. 'Oh, how am I going to get back? We must have come hundreds of miles. Why?' she whispered despairingly.

'You will learn why very soon, *mademoiselle*,' he said, his expression unmoved by the distress of her plea. 'Until then, please do not distress yourself. I assure you, you will come to no harm.'

'How do I know that?' She huddled down, small and cold and frightened.

He made no response, concentrating all his attention on negotiating the pass at the maximum speed possible, and she wondered bitterly why she had been so utterly foolish. She was in a strange country where she knew neither the people nor the customs, her knowledge of the language was nil, even if she succeeded in evading Mahmoud and asking someone for help, and where could she run now that night was so near?

Already the sun was turning crimson, bathing the landscape in fire and painting a fantastic sunset of rose and gold flames across the sky. Was there no end to these miles into the unknown? Frightened, defeated, and aching with weariness after the long hours cramped in the car, Melissa huddled deeper into her jacket as the stars came out across the blue velvet heavens and the car continued to rush through the darkness.

Whether she had passed from the numb apathy of despair into sleep she did not know, but suddenly she was wide awake and aware that engine throb and motion no longer vibrated through her body. Someone touched her shoulder and Mahmoud's voice said: 'We are here at last, *mademoiselle*. Permit me to take your arm lest you stumble in the darkness.'

Her limbs trembling and unsteady, Melissa acquiesced, allowing him to guide her towards the dim blur of a doorway. The faint scents of blossoms drifted to her nostrils and a spark of an idea in her tired brain suddenly told her that the amulet would be above her head as she entered into a dimly lit entrance hall. There were several doors leading from it, and a woman came forward, a plump woman, almost as buxom as Mahmoud, with strands of grey in her dark hair. She wore the dark *djellaba* but no veil, and she motioned Melissa to enter the room from which she had emerged.

Melissa stopped. 'My sister . . .' was all she could manage, and the woman nodded. 'She is waiting for you, *mademoiselle*. But I will bring you refreshment. You will be weary after your long journey.'

Slowly Melissa approached the entrance, passed

45

into a shadowy room filled with the soft glow of lamps on crimson and blue and gold silks, inlaid mother-of-pearl and the gleam of burnished bronze. There was a girl standing in the centre of the room. She was young and fair and slender and she was wearing a mini-skirted dress as brief as Melissa's own. She held out her hands and came forward, and smiled. 'Hello, sister mine. Welcome to Kadir.'

Sister mine!

Melissa jolted to a standstill, shock darkening her eyes and a chill hand seizing her heart. No! She stared at the pale oval face with the flush of pink in the cheeks, the silky corn-gold hair, the beautiful contrast of dark liquid brown eyes, and the smile that frankly challenged, and horror struggled with disbelief.

She put out her hand as though to ward away this fresh shock and stammered: 'But you're not—you're not Avril! You're not——'

'Melissa! Don't you know me? Don't you——?'

'No! I don't!' Melissa fell back, colour draining from her face, trying to fight out of this nightmare. Her voice rose. 'You're not Avril. I—I've never seen you before in my life!'

'Of course you haven't!'

The deep voice came from behind and Melissa turned wildly. The room seemed to sway and blur as she met the dark gaze of the man who had spoken. Her hand fluttered to her throat and she stared at him as though she couldn't believe her eyes.

'*You!*' she whispered soundlessly. 'You!'

The stranger from Casablanca moved like lightning and caught her before she crumpled to the floor.

46

CHAPTER III

'DRINK this—you will soon be all right.'

The jade-green glass misted and receded before her eyes, and the frightening loss of power made the raising of her hand inordinately difficult. She couldn't reach that slender green glass goblet; her hand trembled too much to hold it if she ... The coolness touched her lips and the voice said: 'Drink, slowly ...'

She took a sip of the ice-cold fluid, trying to fight off the strange detachment and the terrifying weakness pervading her limbs. She had never fainted before in her life, not thought faintness was like this. She had always imagined a complete blacking out, then coming round, but not this dreadful helplessness, and being able to remember falling, and then someone carrying her a long, long way, commands being called into the nebulous haze in which she floated ...

The glass was being held insistently against her mouth and the pressure behind her head became that of an arm, urging her head forward. She said weakly: 'It's water ...'

'Of course it is water. You do not need a stimulant. You need rest.'

The glass was moved away, and the voice said incisively: 'Take a deep breath, as deep as you can, and another one, and try not to be so alarmed. You are perfectly safe.'

Safe! A more lucid awareness began to return at

47

last and the assurance in the statement had a completely opposite effect. She blinked and tried to sit up, her frightened gaze roving round the big shadowy room which was utterly strange. A row of three high latticed windows shaped like minarets, a cool scented darkness wafting from them, as though it would enwrap her in its velvety softness, dim shapes of a carved chest betraying pearly gleams hidden amid its panels and an oval mirror above a dressing-table, a rich thick rug stretching beyond the ambience of the lamp nearby, a large amber and bronze lamp spilling a soft glow over the primrose silk cover of the divan on which she was lying, and throwing into the shadowy relief the strong planes of the face of the man looking down on her, in the crook of whose arm she rested. Fear came back to haunt her eyes as she stared up fearfully at the stranger from Casa.

'Where am I?' she whispered. 'Why did you bring me here? She isn't Avril. Why did she say——? Oh, I don't understand! It's a nightmare!' Melissa trembled and buried her face in her hands. 'Why?' she repeated despairingly.

'For many reasons. Too many to begin explaining now.' The stranger stood up and turned towards the door, making a gesture to the woman who had entered silently and stood there before Melissa was even aware of her presence.

The woman came forward and set down a tray on the carved chest, then took the folded garments she had carried over her arm and put them on the end of the divan before she went from the room as silently as she had entered.

The stranger said, 'You have had a very long and

wearisome journey, it is to be expected that you should feel exhausted. It is also unlikely that you will feel inclined to eat, but you must eat a little of this and drink all the milk—it is perfectly safe, from our own herd, I assure you—and then you must rest.'

'How can I rest?' she asked bitterly. 'You tricked me into coming here, telling me that Avril was here, and all the time it was——'

'Avril *is* here.' He swung round and his features hardened into the arrogant lines she remembered. 'You will see for yourself in a moment, when you pull yourself together and calm down.'

'Calm down!' Some of Melissa's fighting spirit returned. 'You expect me to calm down and believe the most arrant tissue of lies I've ever——'

'All right.' He raised one hand and the hard tanned face softened slightly. He came back towards her and looked down into her stormy eyes. 'I know this has all been distressing for you, Miss Blair, but believe me, the shock you received when you arrived was no part of my plan. Far from it,' his mouth tightened, 'and I shall certainly have something to say to the culprits about *that* unpleasant little episode.'

Melissa sighed, the brief flare spent and exhaustion taking its toll again. She said wearily, 'I still don't understand. What do you want of me? What is this plan?'

'You will learn of it—at a more appropriate time. For the moment I must insist that you rest. A car journey of some sixteen or seventeen hours across Morocco does not leave one feeling exactly on top of the world. I know you don't believe me, and I have an accurate idea of the thoughts chasing round under

49

that rebellious expression of yours, but you will have to wait until morning for some of the answers. Now,' he gestured towards the tray, 'when you have eaten that, and not before, I shall send Avril in to see you.'

She looked at the daintily set tray and then at the tall imperious man, and her expression was still bitter with disbelief. 'I—I'm not hungry,' she said.

'Probably not,' he said coolly, 'nevertheless, I shall stay here until you do eat.'

He looked quite capable of enacing the calm statement and reluctantly she picked up the glass of creamy looking milk. She tasted it and some of her misconception vanished; the goat's milk was unexpectedly delicious, not over-rich or strong, or unappetising as she had feared. The two small rolls spread with a savoury cheesy mixture were light and easily assimilated and so were the two crisp little cakes that tasted of almond and honey.

'You see, it was quite easy after all.' His brows went up and his unsmiling mouth was unfuriatingly assured. 'Would you like any more?'

'No, thank you.' She looked away, suddenly wishing she'd refused to eat, wishing she could . . . if only she wasn't so damned weary, as though she wanted to close her eyes and tell the whole world to go to the devil. If only she could summon the strength to defy and challenge and fight this arrogant man who had literally kidnapped her. It amounted to that, the way he'd got her here by false pretences, telling her . . .

'Avril will arrange for you to have anything else you need for the night. Goodnight, Miss Blair, and I trust you will be comfortable here.'

Without giving her time to formulate any reply he

went from the room.

Melissa put her hand to her brow and stared at the closing door. So much had happened she didn't know what to think and her brain was too dazed to chase any longer round the frightening maze of questions that didn't make sense. Only one thing stood out clearly: she wouldn't see Avril. She might as well face the fact. Avril wasn't here and there was some appalling mix-up somewhere. There had to be, unless . . . Melissa's nerve failed her and she began to tremble. That strange girl calling her by name, expecting recognition, expecting her to accept as her sister someone she'd never seen before in her life. *Oh no, is this how it starts?* she moaned softly. Is this how madness begins . . . ?

The sound of the door opening startled her into panic-stricken immobility, almost afraid to look at the slender ash-blonde girl standing on the threshold, pausing and smiling for a moment before she threw up her hands with a gesture Melissa had seen thousands of times. Was it really Avril grinning there, or was it a mirage?

'So you got here at last, Lissa. My word, it's a hell of a run from Casa, isn't it? How's everyone and how's . . .? Lissa! Have you lost your voice? Looking at me as though I'm a ghost. What's the . . .?'

Melissa stood up and was forced to sit down again. The relief of seeing Avril and hearing her voice brought a dangerous return of weakness so that for a moment she distrusted her limbs to obey her command. She shook her head. 'It *is* you, Avril? You're not . . . that other girl . . . Avril, for heaven's sake, what's going on?'

51

'Nothing's going on, darling.' Avril's eyes widened with the innocent look Melissa also knew well. 'But I must say this is a bit of a shock, you turning up like this. Whatever possessed you to come all this way? I got a shock when I heard you were over here.'

'You got a shock! What do you think we got when we couldn't trace you? And you can sit there and say you got a bit of shock.' Melissa took a deep breath, and the return of sanity brought indignation. 'I think you'd better start explaining, Avril. Why did you go off without a word? Without letting us know or having the decency to leave an address where we could contact you. Mother's worried sick about you. And if you knew I'd come to look for you why didn't you get in touch? Instead of . . . What are you doing here? And who's this man who—who practically tricked me into coming here, and . . .'

'Oh, you mean Raoul.' Avril gave a knowing grin. 'He's quite shattering, isn't he?'

'I could think of other descriptions more fitting,' Melissa said tartly. 'He's the most arrogant, ruthless blighter I've ever met, and if I never meet him again it'll be soon enough.'

Avril giggled. 'That's your trouble, darling. You've no guile. I expect you let fly at him and got a shock when you found you didn't have the last word. Honestly, Lissa, you never learn, do you? You just don't try to fight a man like Raoul.'

'I'm not interested in fighting him, I'm only interested in getting home and taking you with me. Thank goodness I'll be able to send that cable at last and let Mum know.' Melissa paused and a new thought struck her. She said sharply 'You're not involved with this Raoul, are you? You haven't done anything crazy?'

Avril shook her head and laughed outright at the horrified suspicion on her sister's face. 'You know me, darling; number one's the important one. It's the only way in this hard cruel world. No, now don't start lecturing me . . .' she said mockingly, 'besides, I'm forgetting, I've to see to my hostessly duties. I see Meriam brought you a nightie and a robe. Trust you to come like a lost weekend. You're the one who needs a keeper!'

Ignoring Melissa's indignant exclamation, she crossed the room to a door Melissa had not previously noticed and flung it open, indicating the interior with an airy wave of her hand. 'You'll find towels and soap and everything you need in here. Meriam will bring you morning tea about seven-thirty, breakfast's any time between seven and nine, depending on how you feel. It's all quite lush, I can assure you. There's a pool, and you can ride if you want to, or just laze around. It's too hot most of the time to do much else. Well,' she stretched and yawned languidly, 'I can go back to bed now, sister mine.'

Melissa turned from her contemplation of an extremely luxurious bathroom fitted throughout in ice-blue and stared at her sister. For a moment words were beyond her, then she almost exploded with wrath. 'Just like that! You can go back to bed! Oh, no, not until you tell me what all this is about. I want to know why you're here—and why *I'm* here,' she added grimly.

'No can—I've had my five minutes already. Rules of the jolly old house, you know,' Avril said flippantly.

'We have to obey orders.'

'Whose orders?' It was a stupid question, Melissa thought helplessly, even as she uttered it.

'Need you ask?' Avril did not seem in the least perturbed. 'He makes the rules around here, darling, and it pays to obey them.'

'And you do?'

'Of course. I do work here, you know.'

'You mean you . . .?'

'I mean I work here, I told you I had a new job. It's dead easy—except for——' She hesitated and shrugged. 'I'm well paid, so I obey the rules. It's as simple as that.' The amusement had died from Avril's face and the cool, hard self-possession was back in her expression. 'I didn't ask you to come here interfering in my affairs, so I'm afraid you've only yourself to blame for what happens.'

Melissa stared. 'What do you mean? What happens?'

'That we don't know—but we will in the morning,' Avril said coolly. 'So for heaven's sake, turn in and stop nagging—you do realise it's three o'clock in the morning, don't you? I'll see you at breakfast—if I'm up by then. Sleep well.'

With this flat rejoinder Avril had gone before Melissa could make any further protest. The echo of the door closing had a strange finality about it, and it had the effect of checking the instinctive steps Melissa took forward. The half-formed idea of stopping Avril, following her to insist on instant explanations, died and her hand dropped to her side. It was dreadfully late and she knew from experience how Avril could close up when the secretive mood took her. Melissa turned slowly towards the bathroom; the main worry was settled; she'd found Avril, and Avril seemed as self-assured and stubborn as ever.

But all the puzzling aspects still remained, and as Melissa went through the mechanical preparations for retiring she found despair superseding the weariness of physical exhaustion. The reunion with her sister had proved totally different from the meeting she had imagined. She had to admit that Avril hadn't seemed exactly overjoyed to see her. She'd evaded answering questions, seemed almost resentful. Why? And what had she meant by obeying the rules? And, even more disturbing on reflection, what had she meant when she said: *'You've only yourself to blame for what happens.'*?

What did Avril expect to happen?

And who was the other girl?

Melissa cradled the soft fluffy blue towel against her face and stared into the wall-size mirror with eyes that were dark with foreboding. There was only one thing which instinct screamed with fatal certainty: the centre of it all was the stranger from Casa. Raoul ...

Shakily, she spread the towel along the gleaming rail and rested her hands on it, knowing only that she wished with all her heart that the answer had lain in anything or anyone other than this particular man. For a moment she was back in time, in a sunlit street in Casa, recognising the underlying character of a stranger; a man who would be an unshakeable ally— or a remorseless enemy. Events seemed to be proving the accuracy of her lightning surmise, even as they failed to provide a single reason why she should be the object of his enmity.

Sighing, she went back into the adjoining room and the discovery she made when she did so turned the tremors of unease into chill, trembling fear.

While she had been in the bathroom someone had secured all the window grilles—and locked the outer door. There was no key.

For the first time in her life Melissa knew what it was like to be a prisoner.

*　　　*　　　*

She experienced many reactions in the minutes following that frightening discovery, the most compelling of them being the frantic urge to scream for release, demand her freedom, find a way of escape.

When she had made certain that there was no mistake, and no way out, the first impact of shock was abating, leaving a cold impotent fury as she realised her helplessness and how useless the blind desire to scream for release. If someone wanted to imprison her they would hardly be likely to go to the trouble of doing so only to meekly release her at her first squeak of rage.

She sank down on the divan and a modicum of sanity prevailed as she faced an unpleasant truth; even if she did succeed in escaping where could she run in the darkness? She had no idea where she was, except that it was a long way from the kind of civilisation she recognised as such, and she had very little money— very little of anything—with her. For the moment she had no choice but to accept that she was helpless, no matter how bitter the despair of that acceptance, until morning brought light and something tangible against which she could fight.

But there was little sleep for Melissa when weariness finally drove her to slide into the cool luxury of pure silk sheets and the softly sprung comfort that at any other time should have wooed her into relaxed, perfect sleep. There was no clock on the little table by the head of the big divan, and many times during the dark hours she cursed the lack of her watch, wished bitterly she'd never strayed into that little street where a small pathetic creature had roused all her instincts for anger and compassion . . .

When the first pale apricot rays tinged the eastern horizon the light came quickly, bringing the shapes in the spacious room to increasing clarity. Melissa stirred, rubbing hot tired eyes, not sure if she had actually fallen into a brief, restless doze. She sat up, the primrose silk covering falling away from her bare shoulders, listening for sound as her wideawake senses warned that someone was at the door.

She called, 'Is that——? Who's there?'

'Oh, you're awake,' said a light voice instantly. 'May I come in?'

'Can I stop you?' Melissa muttered, and threw back the coverlet. The door opened as she did so, revealing a rectangle of primrose-walled corridor and the curve of a large gold and red-lustred jar partly out of her range of vision. The fair girl advanced out of the rectangle and looked at Melissa over the tray she carried while she reached back with a slender sandalled foot to kick the door shut.

She plonked the tray down on the small table and said sulkily: 'There's your tea—I've been sent to apologise.'

Melissa stared at the averted face of the girl who had made her startling announcement of identity the previous night and for the moment did not think of it consciously. She said angrily: 'Was it *you* who locked me in here?'

The girl turned sharply and her sulky expression changed to surprise. 'Locked you in? Me? What are you talking about?'

Melissa closed her eyes; she must have got into a madhouse. 'Didn't you? Somebody locked me in, and I want to know why, and who.'

The girl picked up the small silver teapot and filled the cup. 'You must be imagining things. Nobody locked you in. The door was open just now. There's no key there, and I've no key. Are you sure?'

'I'm sure.' Melissa passed her hand over her brow and reached for the dainty bone china cup. She was beginning to feel unsure of anything. She looked at the girl, who now seemed genuinely puzzled. 'Somebody did, but ... oh, it doesn't matter. Why did you say you were Avril last night?'

'It was a joke. We didn't mean to upset you. We...'

'We?'

'Your sister and ...' the fair girl had the grace to look somewhat discomfited,—'that's why I have to apologise. But we never thought you'd take it like that.'

'You didn't think!' Melissa said furiously. 'Didn't you think I might be worried sick about Avril, not knowing where she was? Where is she?'

'She's not up—need you ask? You raised quite a stir last night, you know,' the fair girl said carelessly,

58

catching sight of her reflection in the dressing-table mirror and flicking at her long silky hair. 'By the way, you'll have to get used to the name-swapping while you're here or you'll ruin everything.'

Melissa's cup went down with a sharp chink, and the brief sense of returning normality vanished. She stood up. 'Listen, what *is* all this? What will *I* ruin? What's the mystery? Who are you?'

'Me?' The hint of mischief returned to the wide, provocative eyes. 'I'm Avril Blair. It's all very sinister. Fun, but sinister. You mean they haven't told you yet?'

'No, but I'm going to find out.' Losing all patience, Melissa snatched the primrose wrap from the foot of the divan and thrust her arms into it. 'There must be someone around who hasn't gone stark raving mad.' The silky folds flared out behind her as she whirled angrily into the bathroom. 'What do you all do here in your spare time?' she demanded over the spurting hiss from the taps. 'Write monster movies, or run the Moroccan M.I.6? Name-swapping. Dragging me half-way across the country. Locking me in. Treating me as though I——' Melissa spluttered and gasped under the unexpected force of a shower spray which she had inadvertently turned on to full spate. Ducking out, she cried, 'I don't know what game you and my stupid sister are playing, but I can tell you it's not funny.'

The younger girl had drifted to the bathroom door while this tirade rushed forth. Apparently unconcerned, she said, 'Try that man's talc—it's gorgeous. I think they're making lusher stuff for *them* than us. Have you ever tried . . .?'

Her mouth tightening, Melissa ignored her, towelling herself roughly dry and grabbing the first talc that came to hand while the high spots of angry colour flamed in her cheeks. She brushed past the girl and looked distastefully at the undies she had worn yesterday and which she had no option but to don again. Her dress was limp and creased and *horrible* after the long day of travelling, and it all added acrimony to the mental argument she was rehearsing for the moment when she confronted the man called Raoul. *He* was behind all this, and when she saw him . . .

She combed her hair impatiently and pinned it back into severe lines, for once caring little that she was devoid of cosmetics. She swung round. 'Now, where will I find him? This man Raoul?'

'Oh, Raoul . . . I meant to tell you . . . he's waiting for you. As soon as you're ready you're to join him for breakfast. I'll show you where . . .'

Just like that! Melissa's anger hardened and immediately she experienced the contrary urge to refuse, to keep him waiting. With an effort she assumed an icy calm and gestured to the door.

There, the girl paused suddenly and stared at her for a moment, then grinned. 'He's really got you mad, hasn't he? He said you were a reckless, stubborn little fire-eater—and an absolute menace he hadn't bargained for. And that——' The girl checked. 'Here's Meriam—we'd better go. Come on.'

The woman who apparently was the housekeeper had paused just outside and looked curiously into the room. She asked for the tray and Melissa managed to maintain control as she responded, but if she had been simmering a few minutes previously she was now at seething point as she followed the other girl. So she was reckless, stubborn, a fire-eater! A *menace*! All this! After—Melissa's hands clenched; there weren't words to express her feelings at this moment.

What she had assumed from one glimpse to be a corridor proved to be a tiny annexe which merely shielded the entrance to the bedroom she had occupied. Its open archway gave directly on to the patio which bordered all four sides of the *riad*, the large enclosed garden, rectangular in shape, around which the house, was built in the traditional Moroccan style.

There were pools and two fountains, and little arbours among the miniature shrubberies, and little winding mosaic paths leading from the long graceful Moorish colonnade edging the patio. It was tranquil and very beautiful, and cool with the fresh sweetness of early morning, but Melissa was blind to its charm and immune to its peace broken only by her own steps ringing a brittle tip-tapping on the mosaic as she followed the longer, more languid steps of the fair girl.

At the first angle joining the long and short sides of the patio the girl stopped and gestured to where the high grilled window shutters stood wide open to the garden a little farther along. 'In there,' she said.

Melissa glanced at her, and the girl waved vaguely and took a pace back. 'Just go in.'

Obviously she had no intention of remaining there any longer than necessary. Melissa gave her another look and took a deep breath. Chin high, she marched along the patio and in through the open french window.

'Good morning!' ·

She jerked to a halt within inches of collision with the tall figure who had moved from the side of the room at the precise moment she entered. She backed a small pace from the broad, white-clad shoulder she'd almost buried her nose into and said coldly, 'Good morning—I was told to come straight in.'

'Oh yes, won't you sit down, Miss Blair. I didn't expect you quite so promptly. Did you sleep well?'

'I didn't—and I'm surprised you even do me the courtesy of asking.' Melissa ignored the satinwood and lime chair he indicated and remained standing. 'But it doesn't matter. I want to——'

'Yes—I'll order breakfast immediately. Do you prefer fresh fruit or juice?' He was brushing past her to touch an old-fashioned bell-push near a large ormolu and lacquer cabinet that dominated one wall. 'Coffee? Or the favourite English tipple?'

'No! I don't want anything. I want to know why I've been brought here,' she flashed. 'I want to know why my sister is here. What hold you have over her. Why you're keeping her here. And why did that other girl say she was——?'

'Calm yourself and sit down,' he said imperturbably. 'I shall answer all your questions—after breakfast.'

'I demand to know now. I——' She gave an angry exclamation as a white-robed servant entered silently and the man from Casa turned away to issue crisp instructions. The dark boy glanced past his master, betraying neither surprise nor curiosity at seeing her there in what was obviously the private domain of the master of the house. When the boy withdrew the stranger turned back to her and his expression had

62

taken on the sardonic air of amusement which infuriated Melissa more than outright rudeness or indifference.

He said: 'It will only be a few moments, and you will argue with more strength on a full stomach. Although,' his mouth compressed slightly, 'you fire extremely well even when hungry.'

Her own mouth compressed. 'Must you be insolent as well?'

'I'm sorry, I did not intend that deliberately. But you are mistaken about several facts. To start with, I have no hold, as you term it, over your sister and I can't imagine how you have gained such an impression. Secondly, she is here entirely of her free will—and receiving adequate remuneration for her services,' he added dryly. 'Thirdly, I hoped I'd made it perfectly clear last night that their foolish prank was no part of——' He stopped as the door swung open and the boy entered with a large tray.

There was silence in the airy room as he deftly transferred dishes from the tray to the small table already laid with white linen and the same delicately patterned china as Melissa's morning tray had held. There was quite an array when the boy stood back and looked enquiringly at his master, then said: 'Three minutes, master?'

'Three minutes, Miss Blair?'

'What?' She stared.

'Your breakfast egg.'

Melissa closed her eyes. This was crazy. Were these the only answers she was to receive; tea or coffee, a three-minute egg? She nodded and sank down in the chair he had drawn out for her. He said, 'I'm afraid I can't offer you *The Times*—except one two days old.'

'I don't want *The Times*,' she said wearily, unrolling the snowy napkin by her side plate, 'I only want . . .' She looked up at him. 'You have too many advantages, and I don't even know who you are, or where I am. Is that to remain a mystery as well?'

He passed her the tall glass jug of orange juice and the silver thermal container packed with ice cubes. 'My cousin and your sister are certainly maintaining discretion. It's Germont—Raoul—if it is not too soon for you to become informal.'

She made no reply beyond the slightest inclination of her head, and he leaned forward. 'Relax! You are sitting there looking as though a tiger might appear at my shoulder at any moment. There is no need to be frightened.'

'What else do you expect me to be?' Nervous now, in a subtly different way from her previous fear, she split and buttered one of the feathery croissants, taking rather a long time over the small task to avoid having to face that disturbing regard. 'You still haven't told me where this place is.'

'This is Kadir. It is very small, too small to warrant an entry in the guide books for tourists—which is the way we prefer it.'

'That is becoming very obvious, judging by the way you——'

He shook his head and she sensed the approach of the boy. A large brown-speckled egg nestling in a yellow egg-cup was set before her, and the sight of that speckled egg seemed to underline the final touch of absurdity. It was so normal, so utterly un-sinister after the escalating chain of events leading to this moment that she experienced the sudden deflation of anti-climax.

In silence, aware now that she was extremely hungry, she finished the egg and two more croissants. There was even a choice of cube sugar and brown sugar for coffee, and chunky marmalade as well as honey beside that folded copy of *The Times* that was two days old. She looked up, met the dark, considering gaze at the other side of the table, and shook her head. 'I still don't understand, *monsieur*, but I enjoyed my breakfast.'

'You look much better now—the English-style breakfast we've had to import for my cousin seems to have reassured you, somewhat.' He flipped open a packet of English cigarettes, and when he had lit hers he rose to his feet. 'Come, I will show you the gardens and we will talk. No, not the *riad*—this way.'

He gestured away from the window by which she had entered and touched her arm as he indicated the other french windows at the far end of the big room.

There was another terrace bordering the outer perimeter of the house. It overlooked informally laid out grounds partially wooded with big spiky shrubs and clusters of stubby palms. A little way along the terrace Raoul Germont turned on to a broad sandy path that wound down away from the house. When they reached the first curve in it he said suddenly:

'How does it feel to be kidnapped, Miss Blair?'

Shock coursed through her. 'So it's that after all! I was right! You *are*——! I *was* locked in last night! She said I was imagining it, but I——'

'You were locked in for your own safety,' he interrupted, 'and for that reason only. Had you decided to

65

try to run out into the night harm might have befallen you. No,' he said grimly, 'I wished you to understand something of the threat hanging over my cousin.'

'Your cousin?' Melissa experienced a fresh wave of surprise. 'Is she——?'

'My cousin Amorel, who played that stupid prank on you last night. But the threats against her are no prank, I assure you. So that is why she is here, and why your sister is here, and—indirectly—why you are now here.'

'But why should anyone want to kidnap her?' Melissa halted, her eyes showing disbelief as she stared at him.

'Why is kidnapping threatened? For gain, as a means of extortion of that gain. The motive is always the same.' He walked on, his steps gritting on the stone-pitted sandy path. 'Amorel is an heiress. She inherits a sizeable fortune when she is eighteen, and owing to certain conditions governing her inheritance I have had to bring her here and take steps to safeguard her.'

Melissa was silent for a moment. Then she said slowly: 'But where do we come into it? We know nothing of your cousin and her fortune, or of you. Why Avril, and why me?'

'Because your sister, having a slight resemblance to Amorel, agreed to take her place for a while as part of my plan to safeguard Amorel.'

The pieces of the puzzle were beginning to fall into place at last—and also some of the implications. Melissa's mind leap-frogged rapidly over them and came to the obvious and alarming conclusion. Again she halted.

'So if any kidnapping is done it'll be my sister who suffers! If they think Avril is ... they'll take her, and ... And you have the nerve to ask her, to expect her to risk her life for a total stranger. How dare you? I've never heard anything so ...'

'Keep your voice down,' he said sharply. 'I trust there'll be no kidnapping, or danger to your sister. Provided *you* try to show a little more control and a little more sense.'

'Sense!' Her hands clenched. 'I think I've come just in time. I've never heard such an inhuman plan. You ...'

He held up his hand. 'Hear me out, please. I have taken every possible precaution to avoid the danger you fear. And all might have been well, until *you* began your investigations. No one knew of Amorel's whereabouts—or your sister's—before you started raising clouds in Casa, asking everywhere, and tracing us to my grandfather's old place on the coast, which meant I had to change my plans and bring them both here. You do realise, don't you, how near you came to ruining all my plans?'

The dark visage filled with imperious accusation sparked her temper instantly and she burst out: 'Yes! And I'm glad I did! You had no right to do such a thing. Well you can find somebody else to do your dirty work. I don't know how you coerced Avril into coming here but it's over now, thank goodness, now I've found her. I——'

'Over?' The word was quietly spoken.

'Of course! You don't think we're staying a moment longer, do you?' Melissa swung round to hurry back towards the house. 'We'll be out of here just as soon as Avril can pack. And don't you dare try to stop her.'

'Just a moment. I'm afraid that's out of the question.'

He had overtaken her with a couple of long strides. She tried to shake free of the hand gripping her arm and said angrily: 'Leave go! You've no right to stop us. You . . .'

'Listen, you little fool. I don't want to hurt you, but you're asking for it. You're here now, and you'll have to stay. There's no alternative. It's only for three weeks, and if you behave yourself it could be a very pleasant holiday. If you . . .'

'Holiday! You must be crazy! As if we would. We're leaving,' she cried, 'and don't dare try to stop us! Or . . .' She stopped and fell back a pace, something in the shake of his head infinitely dangerous.

He said, 'I *can* stop you. And if I fail . . .' He paused and raised one hand, his expression ironical. 'If you will take a mere half-dozen paces, Miss Blair, you will see something which will not fail.'

For a long moment she hesitated, then, despite the angry defiance holding her in its grip, she took the few steps which brought her to a bend in the path and a spur where the ground dropped away sharply and a view opened out that took her breath away.

At the foot of the long steep hillside stretching away below she could see a high wall snaking away to each side as far as she could see; beyond it was a sight she had never expected to see, yet if she had not been so utterly possessed by her anger and own predicament it was the first thing she would have expected. It was gold, dappled with darker billowing ripples where the ascending sun blazed across its vastness, and it stretched unbroken as far as the eye could see, to that shimmering haze where the sky began.

'Yes, the desert,' said the quiet voice at her shoulder. 'Even if you were to escape me, you would not get very far.'

Dismay and the sight of those endless wastes kept her silent, and a new chill crept remorselessly through her entire body.

'There is something else,' he went on in the same chilling voice. 'This is my world. Here, everyone is loyal to me. Loyal to me as they were to my father, and his father before him. Wherever you go, I shall know. Whatever you say, I shall hear. And if you are foolish enough to try to leave I shall bring you back.'

He moved slightly, and slowly she turned to look at him. He was staring across the burning sands and now there was that air of alien affinity she had sensed in him the first time of meeting. Against this setting he was complete.

He said coldly: 'I will safeguard Amorel at all cost, and I will not be thwarted by a stubborn little English miss who would care more for an animal's fate than that of a human being.' He turned then, and the power in his eyes further silenced the defence she still sought to regain.

'If you will try to co-operate I promise to do everything in my power to ensure that your stay here is a pleasant and comfortable one. If not . . .'

He stopped, as though he was letting her read what she liked in his silence, and slowly, feeling as though she were back in the nightmare, she looked back at the desert.

'Why don't you admit it?' she said bitterly. 'You are going to keep me a prisoner here.'

'Prisoner is not a pleasant word, but yes . . . if we must be blunt . . . it is the only way. You will stay here, my prisoner.'

CHAPTER IV

THE copper-hazed dunes shimmered and the arid waves of the sirocco licked greedily across the lush green of the oasis, stirring through Melissa's hair and rousing her from her trance of shock.

The man beside her had not moved, and she could scarcely believe he had actually voiced those chilling, remorseless threats. She said incredulously: 'I believe you meant that!'

'Yes, I meant it. I never waste time on idle words,' he said coolly.

'You're contemptible!' Her hands clenched and she took a step back. 'You're not even civilised.'

The next moment she was seized in a grip that bit like iron into the softness of her arm. His eyes narrowed and his chest heaved with his angry indrawn breath. 'Be careful. Do not try me with those rash accusations; you may rue them.' His tone was infinitely more quelling in its dangerous quietness than it might have been in blustering anger. 'What do you know of our ways and our code? What do you know of *us*? You, who will not listen and who screams before she is hurt.'

With effortless ease he swung her close to him, holding her so that she was powerless to move. The dark angry eyes bored down, their gaze raking her white face contemptuously before fusing with her own. 'So we are not civilised! You were not so ready

71

with your accusations when you needed my so uncivilised aid to deal with the riff-raff of the bazaar. Perhaps, my hot-headed little English miss with the cold heart, I'd better instil a little uncivilised education where it is so sorely needed.'

Her lips parted, wordless now, her will battling against betraying her fear. 'How dare you!' she choked, twisting her arm impotently against his superior strength. 'Let me go!'

The struggling movement brought pain and a gasp she couldn't repress. Suddenly he released her, giving a muffled exclamation of impatience, and she rubbed at the livid marks of his fingers and the scarlet welling about her wrist. 'How dare you?' she choked again. 'You add insult to injury.'

'It is not my wish ever to injure a woman,' he gritted, 'still less to insult her, even when she provokes me. Why do you force me to hurt you? Why do you not . . .?'

'Why? Why . . .? Oh!' Melissa's voice broke, trembled into incoherence. The hard bronzed features blurred into the bronze of the desert behind him and swam in the brilliant haze of her tear-filled vision. Wanting only to escape she backed, turned and ran blindly into the shelter of the palms.

She had no idea where she was running, only that the narrow rough path must lead down to that imprisoning wall, and that somewhere in that wall there must be a gate. As she ran the bitter interchange reiterated wildly through her brain. At the moment she hated Raoul Germont as she had never hated anyone in her life before. How dared he bring her here, trick her, treat her this way? Dare to threaten to make her his prisoner. She'd rather die than let him succeed in his threat.

The high white wall seemed to extend for miles without a break in it, and when she suddenly realised she was within a cool sunless dimness she stopped, grateful for the respite from the hard white heat of the sun, and tried to calm her chaotic emotions. Gradually she reasoned out the fact that the enclosing wall wandered round what must be much larger grounds than she had realised. Also, as she had passed gradually into its shadow, the wall had veered direction without the conventional corner angle, so perhaps it wasn't only part of the house, perhaps it was the boundary of someone else's domain, she reasoned feverishly. Perhaps escape might be easier, after all.

She moved on, coming almost immediately to a small door set deep in the stone. But it did not respond to her eager grapple with its latch and her heart sank; she was still caught in Raoul Germont's domain.

Her dress was clinging to her and sand clung in the crevices of her sandals, making the straps chafe her feet painfully by the time she eventually reached the main gate. She looked through the grille, at the continuation of the driveway snaking its way down the incline towards a small huddle of white buildings. Beyond them was the desert, and before her was a stout chain and a padlock which had nothing of old Morocco about its solid design. Her shoulders drooped, and a soft footfall gritted at her side.

Mahmoud said: 'Is Mademoiselle all right? El Kadir wishes to see Mademoiselle.'

'El . . .?' She frowned. 'How do I get out of . . .?'

'Monsieur Germont, *mademoiselle*. He is concerned lest you walk too far in the sun, *mademoiselle*. He wishes to . . .'

'But I don't!' she flung at him. 'Is that the village?'

'Yes, *mademoiselle*. You will return to the house now, please?'

'Oh—go away!' She was almost beyond reasoning now. Ignoring the Moroccan's soft-spoken protests she turned away and began to hurry up the driveway. She had to find Avril, find a way out of this impasse.

She was hot, weary and in no mood for nonsense when she located Avril's room and found her awake but not out of bed.

'Good heavens!' said Avril. 'Whatever have you been doing? You look like——'

'Never mind what I look like. Come on, we're leaving.'

'Leaving! Have you gone mad?'

'No, but I'm beginning to think you have. Come on, Avril, you can't stay here a moment longer with that impossible playboy sheik, or whatever he is,' Melissa said urgently. 'I don't know and I don't care what all this is about Amorel or whatever her name is, but we're getting out. *Avril!*' she snapped, 'will you move! Do you know what he said? Do you know what he . . .'

'No, darling.' Avril betrayed a flicker of interest. 'What did he say?'

Furiously, Melissa recounted the incident and concluded 'If he thinks he can get away with it he's mistaken. There must be some form of transport we can hire, just to get us to the nearest telephone. Even if it's a camel,' she cried despairingly.

For a moment Avril did not reply, then she swung

74

her feet off the bed and sat on the edge. 'You can please yourself, Lissa, but count me out. I'm staying.'

'Staying?'

'Oh yes. I'll admit it's the back of beyond, but it's only for another three weeks, and it'll be worth it.'

Melissa stared. 'You mean you refuse to leave? Not that you can't?'

'Right first time.' Avril gave her a sharp look. 'You don't think I'm doing all this for fun, do you? In a month's time I shall be going on the spree of a lifetime. A thousand pounds, darling. Think of it! Clothes, clothes, clothes.' She stretched her arms and her oval, dolly-pretty face took on a gleeful complacency. 'I think I'll go on a cruise, a luxury one, and see if I can find myself a wealthy husband. A mod millionaire I could be faithful to. Opportunity only knocks once—if it knocks at all—and I don't intend to miss it this time.'

She stood up, smiling at Melissa's horrified expression, and added: 'Though I'm not sure I might be missing it here. I'm beginning to wonder if Raoul isn't worth a pot-shot. He's pretty well loaded, what with this place and his interests in Casa. Trouble is, it would mean being stuck here most of the year.' She put her head to one side, considering. 'What do you think?'

'That there's no end to your conceit. What is he to you?'

'I've told you—nothing at the moment, but . . .' Avril smiled cockily. 'Now stop whining and try playing him with a little charm instead of spitting like a fury. I know your paddy and your goody-goody little outlook. You'll only ruin everything.'

75

'Well, of all the . . .'

'All right, I know,' Avril interrupted, 'but you've got here and found me and satisfied your curiosity, so you might as well join the party.'

'It seems I haven't any choice.'

'No, you haven't, darling,' Avril said bluntly, 'and take a tip; try not to get on the wrong side of Raoul. He's the power round here and you're a long way from home.' Apparently unconcerned by her own distance from home, she shed her filmy nightdress and stretched languidly. 'Isn't it bliss to be able to go starkers without freezing?'

Melissa sighed. 'You don't change, Avril.'

Her sister laughed and scooped up her wrap as she made for the adjoining shower room. 'I've no desire to.'

The slim figure disappeared and Melissa shook her head. Sometimes she wondered how Avril could be so different in temperament and outlook to herself. Obviously there was neither sympathy nor help forthcoming from her worldly, egoistic sister. She was turning away when the cool voice called above the sound of the shower:

'What's this about you and Philippe?'

'There's nothing about me and Philippe.' Melissa hesitated, standing in the centre of the big rose and white bedroom. 'I went to him first, to find where you'd gone.'

'Oh . . . what did you think of him?'

'He was charming and very helpful.'

There was a giggle. 'He would be. I know Philippe. I hope you didn't take him too seriously.'

'I was too concerned about you to think seriously

about any man,' Melissa said tartly.

'More fool you. Philippe likes English girls. I had him just like that'—the careless snap of the fingers could not be heard but required little imagining—'it's a pity he's richer in looks than goods. I can just picture him coming to your rescue like a white knight on a noble charger.' Avril reappeared swathed in the fluffy pink folds of an enormous bath towel. There was amusement in her eyes as she added, 'How far did he get?'

Melissa's mouth compressed. 'He didn't.'

'Not even a kiss? Poor you.'

'Oh, you're hopeless!'

Knowing expostulation was wasted on Avril, and feeling as though she was beating helplessly against a stone wall, Melissa returned to her own room.

It was all the more infuriating that Avril, the cause of her present predicament, should take this attitude. Was it true that Raoul was paying her a thousand pounds to stay here for a few weeks and impersonate his cousin? Could there be any real foundation in his astonishing pronouncement that she was threatened with kidnapping?

Melissa ceased her restless pacing. If it were true his concern was understandable, and even the startling step he had taken in the attempt to foil the threat hanging over Amorel. But it didn't make his outrageous treatment of herself any more forgivable. He had no right whatsoever to drag her into his schemes and totally ignore her wishes.

She went to bathe her hot face. What was she going to do now? Whatever Avril said she couldn't—wouldn't—stay here. There were a host of new worries to take the place of the main one now resolved with the reunion with her sister. She had to let their mother know. And there was the lesser, but intensely irritating matter of clothes. Her things were still at the hotel in Casa. The bill would be mounting up, they would wonder where she was, and there was Philippe . . .

Melissa replaced the towel on the rail and her expression hardened. She wasn't going to give up so easily. Why should she stay here against her will? A prisoner! All because of an autocratic, domineering suzerain who thought he could bend her to his will.

Strength and determination buoying her spirit once more, she set off in search of him. Surely he would see reason.

There were sounds of feminine voices somewhere within the cool shade of the *riad* and she hesitated, then went on to where the french window still stood open to the patio. The room within was empty, and she walked its length to reach the other window facing the outer terrace.

No one crossed her path as she continued her exploratory way along the terrace till she rounded the angle and reached the front of the house. Two boys in white cotton *djellabas* were working leisurely in the garden and she was about to turn towards the main entrance when she heard the car engine and saw the white car slide to a standstill a short distance from where she stood.

Raoul got out, slammed the door carelessly, glanced at his wristwatch and strode into the house without glancing to left or right. Obviously he hadn't noticed her in the shadows under the colonnade.

Melissa did not stop to examine her impulse. Seconds sufficed for her to dart to the car, grope frantically for the rear door catch and slip into the back. She closed it softly and crouched down on the soft blue carpeting, out of sight, her heart racing like a piston. He had to be going somewhere. It didn't matter where, as long as she could slip away, find a phone, make arrangements . . . thank heaven she'd picked up her bag through sheer force of habit.

In actuality about a minute and a half elapsed before Raoul emerged from the house and crossed to the car, but to Melissa it felt a tension-filled eternity. She had a fearful vision of him opening one of the rear doors, seeing her—she could almost hear his startled exclamation—and venting his fury as he dragged her out . . .

The vehicle responded with small fluctuations to his movements as he settled in and slammed the door, vibration permeated through the smooth springing and communicated to Melissa's limbs as she lay, and the sudden powerful whirr of the cooling fan made her start, then relax gratefully as the cool refreshing air began to circulate in the car. She sensed the speed increasing, and presently the masculine scent of a cheroot drifted to her nostrils. Immediately her nose began to tickle.

She struggled furiously trying to suppress the urge to sneeze. It was ages since she'd wanted to sneeze like this; all a year since she'd had even a cold, and now the tiniest whiff of cheroot smoke wanted to set her off. She burrowed down deeper and tried holding her breath, for no reason at all remembering Pig and Pepper and knowing a hysterical desire to giggle as well as sneeze. Oh, to be like the Cheshire Cat and vanish, leaving only a grin—or a sneeze! Then she forgot Alice and fantasy in the sudden awareness of silence. The car had stopped.

Raoul got out and the door slammed.

After a long minute of listening she raised her head cautiously and ventured a peep through the smoked glass window. A sigh of disappointment escaped her.

A short distance from the car, Raoul was standing with his back to her, talking to a young Moroccan in a blue checked shirt and denims. All around, as far as the eye could see, were date palms, thousands of them.

Melissa sank back, sick with disappointment. It was obviously a date plantation. What if he was merely visiting it, then returning to the house? Her uncomfortable bid would be in vain.

Apparently Raoul had no intention of wasting time. He called something she could not translate as he swung back behind the wheel and a moment later drove off again.

This time he seemed to increase speed considerably. The car bowled along and the road or track unseen soon deteriorated, greatly to Melissa's discomfort. The journey seemed to be going on for hours and now she was aware of the heat from the camshaft, which, no matter how she shifted her position, it seemed impossible to avoid contacting with some portion of her anatomy.

One hope buoyed through the most uncomfortable ride she'd ever experienced; that the end of it must surely lie in civilisation. She longed to look, but resisted the temptation; speeding into the unknown was yet another extension of the timeless limbo the days had been since the loss of her watch. Just as she came to the conclusion that Raoul Germont could exist without food, water and rest, the speed slackened and the car stopped.

There were rustling sounds that suggested he was collecting some package or something from the front passenger seat, then when she least expected it his arm reached over the back of the seat and flipped down the little locking catches in each door. It seemed impossible that he had failed to see her, and when at last she was alone she gave a heartfelt sigh of relief.

She forced herself to wait, to give him time to get clear, before she sat up with the joyous anticipation of seeing streets and houses and people. She looked out and reality made her want to cry.

She was looking at an encampment in the heart of the desert.

A tall bearded man in robe and hood was greeting Raoul, leading him towards the main tent of the *douar* while children and lean dogs milled around and in the shadows beneath the open front of the tent refreshments were being brought in readiness for the guest. The *shaik* turned, gestured to the sky, and Raoul laughed, then they passed into the shadows and several of the children turned their attention to the car.

Melissa groaned. He was going to sip mint tea and exchange news, feast perhaps, and take his time about it, and these children would not depart until the fascination of their game around the car palled and they sought other pursuits. If she moved and betrayed herself they would set up such a commotion and ... Blast! She would pick his visiting day! She was now incarcerated in a prison a great deal worse than that of the house she had fled from so impulsively. Just how unpleasant a prison it was became apparent within a very short time.

Melissa had forgotten the effect of the atmosphere on a car which stood stationary for any length of time in the sun—especially a desert sun. Within a few minutes she was in a pitiable state, and the temperature climbed until the car interior began to resemble that of a furnace.

Her mouth was parched, and her head throbbed unbearably, and she knew she had to have air. Swimming senses invoked panic strong enough to oust the fear of discovery and she groped desperately for the gadget that would wind down the window. Red flecks danced before her eyes with the effort of manipulating the little handle and sickness made her sway unsteadily as she clutched at the window frame and dragged herself up towards the only slightly less hot wafts of air from without.

Dimly she heard shouts and sensed the commotion outside as her fingers slid helplessly away from their grasped object. Striving to hold on to consciousness, she heard the excited piping voices, the deeper one, authoritative, and the sudden silencing of them as the car door swung open and she toppled forward.

For the second time within twenty-four hours Melissa felt herself lifted and carried like a limp rag doll in the arms of Raoul Germont.

*　　　*　　　*

'You are feeling quite recovered now?'

'Yes, thank you,' Melissa responded tonelessly, and

82

stared ahead at the crimson sunset that was staining the desert red.

She was having difficulty in sorting out the confusion of her emotions and her reactions to Raoul Germont. When he had carried her into the great tent and laid her on a soft-woven white rug she had felt bitter shame at her helplessness and a despair that had vanquished her spirit. Solemn, dark-eyed women had fluttered about her, bringing her water and bathing her face and wrists with a cool lotion that smelled faintly of roses. Later they had touched her throat and temples with oil of jasmine and smoothed a soothing balm on the painful marks of sunburn on her shoulders.

The perfumes still lingered faintly, a reminder of a day still tinged with a haze of unreality. Most unreal of all had been Raoul himself. She had expected anger and the icy castigation with which he had lashed her that morning. But he had remained so quiet she had wondered if it was all a dream, until he left her in the care of the Berber women, to rest until sundown, and she had wondered dully if he intended to abandon her there.

But he had returned some time later, asked her if she felt well enough to begin the journey back, and there had been no word of reproach, no furious demand for explanations.

The crimson darkened, merged into violet, became indigo, and Raoul slowed the car to a smooth standstill. He turned to face her. 'Don't ever dare to do such a thing again,' he said between tight lips.

She closed her eyes; was she so foolish as to imagine she could escape either Raoul or his anger? This was delayed retribution. 'I'm sorry. But can't you understand? How can I make . . .?'

'I understand only that your foolish action could have had tragic consequences,' he interrupted. 'If I had not found you and you had lost consciousness you could have become gravely ill.'

'That would have solved your problem—one of them,' she said bitterly, and heard him give an angry exclamation.

'How can I convince you that I mean you no harm? That I'm trying to do what I think best?'

'Yes, I know your cousin is in danger,' she said wearily. 'I can understand your concern, but please don't start all that again. Can't you realise that *our* people are also desperately concerned about us? My sister apparently disappears from the face of the earth, and then I vanish.' She opened her hands with a gesture of appeal. 'I *must* let my mother know we're both safe. To say nothing of the fact of my hotel bill running up. They are going to wonder what's happened to me. And, though I don't expect you to understand *this*—I have nothing to wear except what I have on now. To go two days in this climate without several changes—never mind one—of clothing isn't funny.'

'But I do understand these things,' he said coolly. 'If you had heard me out this morning I would have dealt with all these problems, and saved you all this distress.'

He paused and took a deep impatient breath. 'Will you endeavour to listen to me, now, and without flaring up to match those fiery tresses of yours?'

'Very well,' she sighed, conceding to defeat and the

growing realisation of the power of this adversary.

'First of all,' he leaned back, 'your sister is not nearly as conscientious as yourself, at least in the matter of correspondence. At my instigation she wrote one letter and later a card to your mother, which should have allayed anxiety. It was no part of my plan to inflict worry on your sister's people—if you stop to consider recent events you must realise that a hue and cry over a missing girl was the last complication I wanted. However, to ensure it doesn't occur again I have instructed my agent in Casa to despatch a cable to your mother, announcing your reunion with Avril and that you are spending a three-week holiday touring the country. And you will be writing in a few days. Which disposes of that problem.'

Just like that! Melissa expelled a sigh of annoyance. 'You've got a nerve.'

'Would you prefer me not to consider your mother's peace of mind?'

'No, but . . . It's the high-handed way you've done all this. As though we were puppets you have a right to—to manipulate however you wish. I . . .'

'Because I could not foresee the circumstances of your arrival,' he interrupted. 'Presently, I think you will understand. But first, the problem of your personal possessions. Naturally I will take care of your hotel bill and arrange to have your luggage collected and brought to you, until then I'm sure my cousin will be delighted to help you over the emergency.'

She shook her head to dispel increasing bewilderment. Did he *have* to go to such lengths to maintain secrecy? She turned to him. 'Why? Why must you keep *me* here? I've nothing whatsoever to do with your affairs. Surely you can let me return to Casa and make my way home.' She met his dark gaze with puzzled eyes. 'If you're worried about ... You can trust me. I won't tell anyone of—of all this. How can I cause danger to Amorel? I wouldn't know her enemies if I saw them, so how can I tell them? Even if I wanted to. Which you can't possibly imagine I should want to.'

He sighed, and his expression was grave. 'I don't believe any such thing, but there is a great deal you will need to know before you can judge whether my actions are completely outrageous, or completely justified.' He paused. 'Would you care to walk a little before we drive on?'

'In this?' Somewhat startled, she glanced at the limitless wastes of dark rippled dunes.

'I know the desert. Do not fear, you are perfectly safe. Provided you do not do anything so foolish as trying to run away,' he added sharply.

'My running-away days are over for a long time,' she said dryly, getting out of the car and standing doubtfully by the glow of the headlights. 'Aren't you going to switch them off?' she asked. 'Your battery ...?'

'The lights are our beacon, and I carry a spare, always.' He came to her side and put a guiding hand under her elbow. 'This way.'

She was still wary of him, but her chastening experience of the afternoon and her increasing awareness of her puniness against the alien desert was more than enough to counterbalance that first wariness; for the moment, Raoul Germont was the lesser of the two proverbial evils.

Their long shadows danced ahead as they walked slowly down the brilliant spill from the headlights, and she remained silent, sensing the man at her side marshalling the pertinent facts he was about to impart. At last he said: 'How much have they told you?'

'Nothing,' she said with some surprise. 'Except in riddles.'

He forbore to comment on this. 'You'll have surmised that Amorel has spent most of her life in England.'

'I thought she was English.'

'Her father is English and she's lived in England since she was three years old, but she was born here at Kadir. My grandfather loved her; she was easily his favourite of us all and he was bitterly disappointed when her father found he couldn't settle here, partly because he never became acclimatised to the dry heat —away from a colder clime he suffered perpetual enervation—and partly because of pressure from his own family. Unfortunately, my Aunt Martine, who made a point of returning home at least once each year, bringing Amorel with her, was killed in a car crash three years later. Jack was drawn back completely under his family's influence—they never approved of his marriage to Martine—and my grandfather never saw Amorel again. He was too proud to beg them to send the child to see him, and too stubborn to make the journey to England, a country which, with due respects to your nationality, Miss Blair, he never loved.'

Raoul stopped to get cigarettes out of the pocket of his still immaculate white shirt and offered her one. When they were lit he went on: 'My grandfather died three months ago. He left Kadir to me, the house and the plantation, knowing I would continue to adminster it in the way he wished, and the bulk of his personal fortune he left to Amorel. But there were certain conditions she had to fulfil. First, she had to be resident in Morocco when she attained the age of eighteen, secondly, she could not transfer the capital anywhere abroad, thirdly, there is a retainer that if she marries without my consent before she is twenty she forfeits everything, and finally, should she fail to fulfil these conditions, the money is to be divided among the other members of the family. Half to myself, and half to Jules, my father's younger brother.'

He stopped and turned to face Melissa, and now she could perceive his deep-rooted concern. 'Can't you see the invidious position in which I am placed? Should anything happen to Amorel I stand to gain, and this is why I'm determined that Jules shall not succeed in his aim. He almost succeeded the first time, but he shan't succeed a second time.'

The vehement anger was back in Raoul Germont's entire mien, the same scarcely controlled force which had been directed at her earlier that day. But now it was not for her. She said slowly: 'This Jules, he must be her uncle. Surely he wouldn't harm his own niece?'

'I believe he would.' Raoul resumed his slow, evenly paced stroll. 'It is too long a story of family contention to bore you with, but if he can prevent Amorel from fulfilling the conditions he will. He has only to remove her from Morocco for one vital day to invalidate the will and he can claim what he thinks is his right. He has much to gain and nothing to lose.'

At last Melissa was convinced that the shadows behind this strange affair held reality after all, and she felt her doubts regarding Raoul Germont's motive begin to dissolve. There was no question of his complete sincerity.

She said, 'You spoke of his almost succeeding. In which way?'

'The day my cousin set out from London, an attempt was made to kidnap her at the airport. Unfortunately for Jules, they got the wrong girl, there was an enquiry and a feeble excuse of it being a student prank, a practical joke. But we know it wasn't.'

Melissa shivered. This was the very incident which her mother had recalled the night before she set off in search of Avril. She remembered laughing at her mother, saying these things didn't happen to ordinary people . . . was anyone ever an ordinary person?

Her sympathies had undergone a swing during Raoul's account, and she could almost forgive him for his high-handed treatment of herself.

As though he sensed this he turned his head and asked: 'You are not thinking quite so ill of me now?'

'No,' her eyes were thoughtful, 'but if only you'd explained in the first place, instead of . . .'

'There was no time. Jules arrived in Tangier with his son last week. We had been staying at a friend's home at Al Hoceima, and there, unfortunately, your sister was recognised by an acquaintance of hers. I contemplated staying in the old summer home outside Casa—we rarely visit it now. After my grandmother died my grandfather could not bear to return there. We . . .'

'Is that the house of the amulet Avril visited? Where . . .?'

He nodded. 'I was there one afternoon when your sister decided to explore. Later I met her again at

89

Sonia's villa.'

It was beginning to tie in now. Melissa stayed silent, and he continued:

'When you began to make your enquiries I became worried. If you had remained alone I would have arranged for Avril to visit you, but you had involved Philippe St Clair, and I did not know how many others. When you traced us to the house at Casa I had to take action quickly, and I decided the best way to ensure safety for Amorel and your sister was to have you brought to Kadir as well.'

The delicious cool of the desert night became chill. Melissa shivered again, and he said quickly: 'You are cold. We will return to the car—you can see Kadir some other time.'

At her look of puzzlement as she halted obediently, he gestured carelessly. 'Over that rise is Kadir. It is a picture of which I never weary, particularly as the moon rises.'

'Oh ... But I'd like to see ... I thought we were still miles away.'

Without speaking he turned again, and was silent until they left the dimly marked track and surmounted the long curving ridge. The sand was soft and shifting, and filled her sandals, but she forgot the impulse to shake and wriggle her toes as they reached the crest and she saw the panorama across the dark desert.

It was almost too beautiful to be real; an exotic stage cut-out of moonlit white roof-tops, a pearly domed minaret of the mosque, fringed by the dark silhouettes of palms and set against a sky so rich it was like a blue velvet backcloth strewn with silver glitter. But it was real, and so was the spell that overtook

Melissa at that moment, to cast an enchantment she knew she would remember all her days. This was desert magic.

Very quietly, Raoul said: 'Will you stay—willingly? Accept my hospitality and see the true Morocco?'

'I—I don't know ... It's so beautiful I can't believe in it.'

'Then you must stay until you do believe. After all, why return after a mere day or so? Two days which have brought distress to you, and for which I should like to make amends.'

Bemused now, she could not reply, knowing if she did it would hold an assent filled with fervency she still wanted to withhold. She had known Raoul's arrogance, his irony, his anger and his ruthlessness; now she was experiencing his charm and persuasiveness, and her own readiness to be swayed was disturbing.

Suddenly he looked down at her and his gaze willed her to raise her own to him, to be held unswervingly. He said softly: 'You are not still afraid, surely?'

The final silken thread of the mesh of enchantment was spun. She said unevenly: 'You make it very difficult for me to refuse. Yes, I will stay—and I am *not* afraid,' she added in the faintest whisper of defiance.

'Good, then we will consider it settled.'

Briskly he took her arm and turned her towards the distant lights of the car. The calmness of his reply came as anti-climax, unexpected. Melissa quickened her steps to keep pace with his long strides down the slope. Anti-climax to what? What *had* she expected ...?

CHAPTER V

THE strain of the past two days overtook Melissa suddenly that night and she fell into a heavy sleep the moment her face sank against the cool silkiness of her pillow. She had no recollection of her sleepy response when Meriam brought her tea the following morning and the next thing she knew was Avril tugging the sheet back and shaking her into wakefulness.

'Come on, Lissa,' she cried impatiently, 'you're holding us up.'

'Me? How?' She rubbed her eyes and sat up. 'What time is it?'

'Nearer ten than nine. Will you come and sort out what you want? Clothes, you dumbcluck,' she added in the same tone. 'Your own stuff won't be here before tomorrow. Lucky we're about the same size—and Amorel says you can help yourself to hers, seeing that it's all in a good cause.'

Still not completely awake and aware of the sense of unreality creeping back—she was still here!—Melissa shrugged into her wrap and adjourned to her sister's room.

'I feel more like the beggar at the feast every moment,' she said with not very good grace when she had selected the minimum of what she would need for the day from Avril's decidedly extensive wardrobe.

Her sister merely shrugged, but Amorel smiled, showing much more friendliness than she had the

92

previous day. 'You'd better borrow some of my sun-cream,' she said. 'With your fair skin you'll burn out here if you don't watch out.'

Melissa was aware of this already. Being a redhead she had the delicate creamy fairness that tanned reluctantly but glowed readily—and painfully. She murmured her thanks, and the younger girl added: 'If you get a move on you can have your fortune told.'

'Fortune?'

'The local sand-diviner. We got Meriam to send for him this morning—he's super.'

Avril's mouth curved cynically. 'She's had her sand read three times since we got here—and believed every word of it.'

'So did you.'

'All that guff about the desert calling her home!'

Despite Avril's scornful teasing it was plain that a certain amount of friendship had grown between the two girls. Amorel merely laughed and said, 'Anyway, he's far better than the horoscopes in the mags at home, and it's something to do. We'll be down by the pool—I'll bet he'll surprise you.'

Would he? Melissa had her doubts. A session with a fortune-teller was the last thing that appealed in her present mood. She went to shower and dress, then ate a light breakfast, alone except for the silent boy who had served the previous morning.

There was no sign of Raoul Germont, nor was there any indication of his presence when sheer loneliness sent her in search of the other two. She found them by the pool, which though small struck an instant note of freshness, completely shaded as it was by thick clumps of tall palms. On a small tiled terrace at one

93

end the sand-diviner was squatting, a thin square of board on the ground before him and the two girls sitting enrapt as he bent over the thin film of sand.

'He must mean Larry,' Amorel was saying. 'He's the only man I know who can pluck music from the air. Well, he does play a guitar—though not very well,' she giggled.

'Ask him if he's past, present or future,' said Avril.

But the dark-visaged seer was impassive. He smoothed out the sand with a decisive movement of obliteration and reached for the piece of cloth at his side. 'The sand will not speak to those who disbelieve,' he said with finality, tipping the sand on to the cloth and drawing the thong to enclose it. Obviously the hour of prophecy was over.

'I told you not to laugh. You know it . . .' Amorel turned her head and saw Melissa. 'Come on—you're just in time to learn your fate.'

'No, thanks.' Melissa took a step back. 'I'd prefer to remain in ignorance of . . .' Her voice tailed off as the sand-diviner's gaze rose to her face. He stretched out a thin bony hand, but the gesture held none of the whining supplication of the professional touts she had seen at the tourists' haunts. There was authority in it, and the proud, burning eyes held an intensity that invoked a shiver in her.

He said, 'The *lalla's* fate is written, even though she is denying it, and will deny it against the truth of the sand.'

The lingering smiles faded from the faces of the other two girls. They stared as Melissa went forward slowly and almost against her will looked down at the handful of sand the diviner cast across the board.

He went on in the same remote tones: 'You have come from afar, into darkness through the day and clouds across the night. There is much darkness and fear for the *lalla*, but it comes not from the desert you fear, nor from the destiny you deny. Hear not the voices you trust, and take not that which is not your own, for the desert veils the hand of *Kismet* who holds the key to the freedom you seek.'

With deliberate care he scattered the fine sand and traced a strange design with a small pointed stick. He bent over it, and Melissa caught her breath in a sigh.

'I—I don't understand,' she faltered. 'Whom must I trust and what am I not to take?'

'It is not always given to mortals to understand.' He looked up at her and there was finality in his grave features. He stabbed at the sand. 'There is the talisman. Take it and do not fear the darkness. The talisman is the key.'

'What talisman?' She shook her head. 'What do you mean?'

'It must remain hidden. Nothing can quell the course of destiny. Look back not upon the sea of night and step upon the sands of the morning. Allah be with you. You will not step alone.'

Silence held the girls in its grip while the diviner gathered together his things and stowed the small drawstring bag of sand beneath the white robe. He touched his forehead gravely, 'Peace be with you, *insh'Allah*,' and in moments was gone.

There had been a strange dignity about him, and a conviction that still held Melissa in its spell, try as she might to free herself.

Avril gave a small choked laugh and said, 'What on

earth was all that about? He never said anything like that to us.'

Melissa shook her head, and Amorel frowned. 'It gave me the shivers—I'm glad it wasn't me. I wonder what he meant by talisman and key. Could you see what he drew?'

Melissa was still silent, puzzled. At last she said: 'I don't think he meant a talisman or key. They were his symbols of prophecy, but they could mean anything—goodness knows what!' she exclaimed with a lightness that wasn't quite genuine. 'But at least it's a change from the dark handsome stranger and news from across the sea sort of thing.'

'It was a kind of warning, though, I felt it.' Amorel frowned. 'I'm sure he was trying to tell you something.' She ignored Avril's scornful exclamation and a light came into her eyes. 'I know! We'll ask my cousin. He'll know. He understands their symbolism —he should do, he's . . .'

'Not Raoul,' Melissa broke in sharply. 'No, please don't ask him, for heaven's sake. He . . .'

'And what must she not ask me?'

He had approached unheard, immaculate in riding kit and his dark head still ruffled by the desert winds. There was a note of indulgence in his voice for his young cousin, but cool enquiry was in the dark gaze resting on Melissa's flushed face.

Amorel chose to ignore the pleading glance Melissa threw at her and proceeded to recount—almost verbatim—the diviner's words.

He listened in silence, the curve of his riding crop tapping lightly against one gleaming leather boot. 'And you take this seriously?' he remarked when she had finished.

'No, of course not.' Melissa's mouth tightened, and she turned away, aware of a feeling of uncomfortable heat. Choosing to blame it on the increasing temperature of the morning instead of the effect of Raoul Germont's sardonic appraisal, she slipped off the light jacket as he said:

'You are wise to dismiss such fancies. After all, what danger here could arouse your fears?'

'None, *monsieur*.'

'But somebody's been arousing the bruises—look at your arms!'

In the silence after Avril's sudden observation Melissa felt as though the marks on her arms were burning like brands for the world to see. From childhood she had become resigned to the unfortunate fact that she did bruise easily, but never before had she hated that fact, and Avril's sharp eyes, as much as that moment.

'I—I bumped myself on—on something.' Angrily she shouldered back into the jacket to hide from sight those marks of Raoul's force the previous day and turned away, almost running to escape back to the house.

'Hey! Aren't you going to swim?' Amorel called.

'Later.' Breathing hard, Melissa returned to her room. When she had cooled down a little she sat on the edge of her bed and stared resentfully at the brilliance of the blossoms beyond the dark, lattice-lace oblong of the window. The scents of rose and orange-blossom drifted faintly into the room, but they brought her no pleasure.

How was she going to stand three weeks of this?

97

Avril seemed perfectly happy—her mercenary little soul was being well greased, she reflected bitterly—and Amorel seemed to treat life as a joke—which she could afford to, with a fortune at the end of three weeks and a cousin-cum-self-appointed-guardian who was going to make sure she got it, ruthlessly sure. But what do I get out of it? Melissa asked herself despairingly. The livid imprints of a man's hands and a situation so mortifying as to be unbearable.

Trying to control her anger as common sense told her that she could only hurt herself by giving rein to it, she wandered to the window and stared through the grille at the peaceful *riad*. It could have been the holiday of a lifetime. For the house on the edge of the desert lacked nothing in sybaritic comfort and its setting evoked a certain atmosphere that stole upon the senses against all resistance of will. Yes, there was a magic about Kadir . . .

Abruptly she turned away; it was a magic she would prefer to leave as soon as possible. The holiday was a prison sentence; and the host was her gaoler.

Suddenly an angry impulse sent her to Avril's room. There was no sign of her sister, and uncaringly she opened the wardrobe and took out a blouse she had passed over earlier that morning. It was flame-coloured cobwebby lace, a colour that needed courage to wear with her colouring, and it was semi-transparent, but it had long sleeves and so would serve her purpose. There was a white piqué skirt which wasn't an ideal complement to the blouse but more acceptable than the flame silk trousers that completed the ensemble on Avril, and she took them back to her room and changed. That done, and by now quite

98

aware that she was sulking and unrepentant of that fact, she found a shady pergola seat in a secluded part of the *riad* and settled down to read until lunch time.

During that meal she remained polite but distant while Raoul, apparently in a good humour, played the perfect host and treated Avril and his cousin as though they were his dear and precious V.I.P. guests. Avril immediately noted the blouse, but forbore to comment, except to remark enigmatically 'Where's the rest of it?' as they moved out on to the patio for coffee.

Melissa merely shook her head. She wanted the lazy toying with after-the-meal drinks and cigarettes to be over so that she could escape the undercurrents of unease that held her tense when Raoul Germont was present. She thought of the sand-diviner, and already the mental disturbance of those moments were disappearing, to be replaced by a new mood of irony. The dawning fear now was that of boredom! Melissa was by nature an active person. Lazing around had never appealed to her, but it seemed that a long session of lazing around was to be her fate—if Raoul had his way. Whatever did they do with themselves all day? There was a limit to the time one could spend reading, and to lie around in this sun was to court heatstroke. She was about to make her excuses and leave the little group when Avril stretched languidly and looked at Raoul.

'My little sister's bored to tears already. What are you going to do about it?'

'Are you, Miss Blair?' The tawny lights glimmered in his dark eyes. 'We must remedy that. What would you like to do?'

She had the feeling he was laughing at her, even though his lean features were gravely composed. 'Does it matter what I want?' she said bitterly.

'But of course,' he said smoothly, 'provided it is within reason.'

'Your reason,' she countered, and looked away.

There was a cold little silence, then Amorel said: 'We could go to the *souk*—it's *el khemis* today. See,' she grinned proudly, 'I'm learning the right days already.'

'It will be hot and dusty,' Raoul said.

'So what? I adore the *souks*. Oh, please, Raoul.' She got up and skipped to his side, putting one arm round his shoulders and looking down into his face with a wheedling expression.

'But Raoul doesn't love the *souks*—sniffing around the perfume-blender, and that character with those ghastly snakes.' Avril shuddered. 'I'm sure Raoul can think of something more entertaining.'

Avril's approach was totally different from that of the younger girl, and the gaze she directed at Raoul was openly challenging. 'Well, what about it?' she added when he did not immediately reply.

'Then we could go on to that place in the hills,' Avril broke in. 'It's a gorgeous drive.'

Raoul gently disengaged himself, leaning forward to stub out his cheroot. 'I do not think Melissa is feeling inclined to take any more drives with me. Mahmoud shall take you to the *souk*. The other can wait.'

'You can count me out,' Melissa stood up quickly, 'I don't feel inclined to drive anywhere at the moment.'

If they thought she was going to fawn on Raoul

Germont for favours they could think again, even if it meant voluntary incarceration within the house's limits, she thought, casting a baleful glance at the amulet above the doorway as she entered. That crack about not feeling inclined to drive with him . . .

She did not revoke her decision, even when Amorel pattered along the terrace and looked in at the open grille, to probe into Melissa's refusal. She hovered a moment, studying Melissa with some anxiety.

'You're still furious with Raoul for bringing you here, aren't you? I'm sorry, it's all my fault. I—I wish he hadn't . . .' She stopped, then after a glance along the terrace came into the room.

'Melissa . . . can I talk to you?'

'Of course.' Melissa looked puzzled, wondering what was causing the sudden change to anxiety in the younger girl. 'It isn't *your* fault. I don't blame . . .'

'No, it isn't that. It's just that I've got to talk to sombody and I . . .' She took a deep breath and sat on the edge of the divan. 'It's not easy to explain. It all seemed tremendous fun, at first, coming out here and the will and everything. We never dreamed that Grandfather would leave it to me, and with all these funny conditions . . . Raoul did tell you, didn't he?'

When Melissa nodded, she went on in the same nervous little voice, almost as though she was afraid of being overheard: 'Grandfather—my English one— was furious. He didn't want me to come here at all, but I talked him round, and after he'd talked to his own solicitor and made enquiries he found it wouldn't be possible to upset the will, not unless I fulfilled the conditions and waited until I was twenty. After that he reckons no one could stop me doing what I liked with

101

it or living where I liked—and believe me, the old place at home could do with a shot in the arm.' A trace of flippancy came into Amorel's face. 'Ever seen a small and seedy stately home? In winter we put all the perishable furniture into the big drawing-room because it's the least damp and we freeze in the room next to the kitchen until spring comes, and last year we had the front painted—no one sees the back.'

Melissa gave a sympathetic murmur, not sure where all this was leading, and said: 'These old houses bring a lot of problems.'

'It isn't that, though. When you came it made me realise how serious it is. At first it was a tremendous giggle, having Avril here and pretending to be each other, but when Raoul brought you here and forced you to stay I began to think of all the other angles. He's determined to make everything happen the way Grandfather wanted it. My making my home permanently here, and then . . .' She bit her lip and looked down. 'I'm not sure I want it to happen that way.'

'Yes,' Melissa sighed, 'it's difficult when one has two countries which are both home.'

'No, you still don't understand. It's Raoul. You see, my grandfather used to write to me regularly all the time I was in England. He used to tease me that I'd come back to my proper home the moment I'd grown up, and then I'd stay for ever, because Raoul would marry me.'

'Oh. Are you going to marry Raoul?'

'No, at least I don't think so.' Amorel got up restlessly. 'I never took it seriously. I hadn't seen him since the last time he visited England when I was fourteen, and I hardly knew him. I didn't want to marry him—I'm half engaged to Larry Denton already—and I'm sure he didn't want to marry me. But there's something about Raoul. Do you know what I mean? When I'm with him I forget about Larry and feel like flirting, just to see how Raoul reacts.'

'And does he?' Melissa asked dryly.

'N-not in the way Larry would. He just smiles and makes me feel like a little cousin.'

'You'll forget about it when this is all over.' Melissa smiled reassuringly. 'It's just with being here with him all the time and cut off from everyone else.'

'I suppose so.' Amorel still looked troubled. 'I wish I knew what was going to happen. Sometimes I long to be home again, then I remember that this is my home as well, and I feel terribly torn. I mean, I couldn't stay here, could I?'

'If you married Raoul you'd have to.'

'But if I didn't . . . I wish I knew what he was going to do. You see, I can't get married without his consent—unless I chuck it all up and go back to England. He mightn't let me marry Larry.'

Melissa shook her head. She was beginning to see that Amorel had her problems, but she still didn't see why Amorel should be so uncertain about her own state of heart. If she loved this Larry enough nothing, not even the redoubtable Raoul would stop her. It wouldn't stop me, Melissa reflected. She said lightly: 'It'll work out. Don't worry. Nobody can make you marry anybody you don't want to marry, or live where you don't want to live.'

'No, you still don't understand, any more than your sister does,' the younger girl said sadly. 'It's easy to be definite when you're looking on.'

'I'm sorry, I do understand,' Melissa said quickly. 'But I'm sure Raoul wouldn't try to stop you marrying this boy if you're really in love with him.'

'But that's just it. I'm not sure any more. That's what I'm trying to tell you. But you're just the same as Avril. She doesn't believe in love. She says you can fall for any man provided he's attractive enough and strikes the right spark. She says it's just physical magnetism that makes you fall for a man, and then you get used to each other and it all wears off. And that's why I'm . . .'

'You don't want to take any notice of Avril. She's always been the same. One of these days she'll fall with a bump and settle down, but for goodness' sake don't be influenced by her opinions.' Melissa regarded the younger girl for a moment, then smiled faintly. 'Avril just wants to enjoy herself at present, but she doesn't mean half of the things she says.'

'Maybe not, but she's right about the attraction bit. That's what frightens me.' Amorel went slowly towards the terrace and the droop of her shoulders betrayed her youthful vulnerability. By the grille she stopped and turned round. 'You see, she's immune to Raoul, and so are you. But I'm not.'

Quick footsteps sounded outside and Amorel turned as the impatient, 'Oh, there you are!' came from Avril. A moment later Avril was also framed against the light. She looked into the room.

'Still in retreat? Don't run away before we get back —you'll only get lost.'

'I won't.' Melissa returned the ironical wave and did not move until silence settled again. Then she paced slowly across the room.

Her initial resentment of the prank Amorel had played that night of her arrival was forgotten now. It wasn't all fun being an heiress, especially one dependent on the authority of a man like Raoul Germont. For a moment her mouth curved wryly. So Amorel had discovered he was attractive, and the attractiveness wasn't quite cousinly, on her own part, anyway. Heaven help her if he decided to exert that attractiveness. A wiser girl than Amorel would resist any dangerous temptation to flirt. . .

The wry little smile flickered again; it was a relief to know *she* was immune . . .

She tried to dismiss the matter and went in search of Meriam to request writing paper. This done, she settled down to write a long letter to her mother. It took more difficulty to compose than she had anticipated, and a small sense of impatience warred with her instinctive avoidance of pouring out the whole story. She was committed now to a certain course of action so she would have to go through with it. If her mother had the slightest suspicion that all was not as it appeared on the surface there would be hell to pay. She re-read it critically, decided it convinced and allayed concern without giving anything away, and slipped it into an envelope, but did not seal it—Avril might want to add a note.

At that point Meriam arrived to enquire if she wanted tea. There was still no sign of the others returning, doubtless they would be late, and she took the tray into the niche she had discovered in the *riad*. When she had succumbed to the temptation of the last of the delicious little honey and almond cakes she relaxed back, listening to the soft deep drone of the bees, and found herself thinking of Philippe St Clair.

She should let him know she had found Avril and that everything was all right—almost all right! she amended. He might be wondering what had happened to her, perhaps even making enquiries. And he'd been very kind, trying to help when she hadn't a single person to whom to turn. Yes, she should let him know . . .

The letter had to be headed simply: Fez, Wednesday, as was her mother's, and followed by the same 'moving on tomorrow' excuse. Melissa's eyes hardened with a cynicism normally foreign to them; she was becoming quite adept at skating over veracity: she was also beginning to experience surprise at her own deviousness once she stopped to reflect on it. It was perfectly understandable when it was for the sake of her own sister, and even for a girl who had been a stranger until two days ago, but that she should lie for Raoul Germont . . . She couldn't quite credit herself, or admit that his power had daunted her spirit . . .

The sunset rose was deepening against the indigo lace shadows stretching from the arbour, telling her that night was very near as she slipped the letter into an envelope and sought in her pocket diary for the scribbled address of Philippe's office. She was capping her pen when the crunch of footsteps came and Raoul looked down at her.

'So this is where you hide.' He appeared to be in a good humour as he seated himself casually at her side. 'You've been alone here, ever since lunch?'

'Yes, but not hiding.' She sealed the envelope and reached for her bag, intending to drop it in beside the one for her mother. But before she could do so he said sharply:

'Did I see right? That letter—it's to Philippe St Clair?'

'And what if it is! Why shouldn't I write to Philippe?'

'No reason at all—in normal circumstances.' His features had reverted to their cold arrogance. 'But these are not normal circumstances. I do not intend to encourage visitors, particularly amorous young Frenchmen. I must ask you to tell me the nature of the message you are sending him.'

'And if I don't?'

'You will leave me no choice but to resort to other methods.'

'Such as those of yesterday morning,' she flared. 'Methods you know I can't counter. How despicable can a man get? You're just a barbarian! Using sheer brute strength——' Her words died in a gasp as he seized her arm and swung her to face him.

'Can you not be reasonable? Must you always provoke?' His face came close and a thin gleam of gold sparked and swung at the open neck of his shirt. He gritted, 'I am many things, but no one has called me despicable and failed to regret it.'

'You are despicable! Let me go!' With her free hand she reached down to the two letters in the open bag. 'Here!' she cried wildly. 'Take them. Read them. Go on!' She thrust them at him, her face taut with scorn. 'Then perhaps you will take my word that they contain nothing to endanger your plan or your cousin's inheritance, or anything! Then you will see why I call you despicable. Well,' her voice rose, 'you've got what you wanted. Why don't you read them?'

He stared down at her, his mouth a grim line as she sank down on the arbour seat and turned her head away.

Her limbs were suddenly dangerously weak and the iron pressure of his fingers still ached in her flesh. She heard the thin rustle of notepaper and knew a flash of bitter satisfaction that it was now almost too dark for him to discern the writing. Then the two letters were put on her lap, the seal on Philippe's still unbroken.

He said quietly, 'I apologise. I misjudged you. But why do you antagonise me this way?'

'Why?' She straightened wearily. 'Ask a silly question . . .'

'I am not accustomed to such antagonism from a woman. Is it any wonder it evokes a similar response?'

'No, not if you treat them like this.' Unconsciously her hands had gone to enfold her arms. 'Force tends to beget force.'

'As pain begets pain. I think I understand.' He reached across and withdrew her arm from its safeguarding clasp. 'I remember now. You said you had knocked yourself on something, this morning.'

He pushed the blouse sleeve up from her wrist and touched the dark bruise shadows on the opalescent skin. 'Did I do this?'

'You did.' She wanted to snatch her arm from his grasp, before her strength was spent completely in the insidious power of this new gentleness, and knew it was too late. One more moment of rash misjudgement would tip her over the borderline of tears.

'But it is not the cause of your pain, I think. You

108

are bitter because you can't lash out with equal force to appease that anger of yours.'

'Do you expect me to submit tamely?'

He shot her a sharp look, his grasp warm and firm still about her wrist, then shook his head. 'No, I think not. Submission in a woman can be extremely boring.'

'Because it doesn't appease your domineering instinct?'

'No, because a submissive woman lacks spirit. Thus she is uninteresting.'

The riposte had flashed like lightning and he was smiling now, his white teeth glimmering in the shadowy planes of his mouth. She realised that the violet veil of the brief dusk had fallen almost unnoticed. Suddenly she was aware of its quality of isolation, and that it had enfolded her in a subtle intimacy with him.

She stirred uneasily, wondering if she imagined his touch becoming more insistent and the outline of him closer to her. She said, 'You can't have it both ways. I suppose you prefer to browbeat a woman into submission to your will.'

'Melissa, what strange ideas you have of me.'

It was the first time he had used her name, and its tones lingered like a caress. A tremor ran through her; the way he had spoken it had penetrated right through the barrier she was striving to maintain against him.

He added softly: 'If I desire a woman's submission I do not have to browbeat her into it. Believe me, there are far more pleasurable ways.'

Warning bells clamoured in Melissa's brain, too late with their message of escape. The essence of Raoul Germont was a tangible power stealing about her, heightened unbearably by the warm heady stillness of encroaching night. She could well imagine the more pleasurable ways ... if a girl was foolish enough to fall for them ... She tried to keep her voice cool as she said: 'For you, no doubt. Now,' she strove to appear practical, 'it's getting quite late. I ...'

'Late? What does time matter?' He was on his feet, placing an escorting hand under her elbow. 'Come, I will show you our English garden.'

'Oh ... but I've already explored the gardens.' She hung back. 'They're all very beautiful, but ... it's dark now,' she faltered hopelessly.

'This is the best part of the day—and you have not explored this particular part of the garden.' He looked down at her, and that disturbing smile glimmered again. 'What's the matter? You are not afraid, are you?'

'Of course not!'

Chin high, she could do nothing but allow him to escort her along the winding path through the *riad* until they reached the house. They passed through a little passage-way she had not known existed and emerged on the outer patio. A little way to the right there was a high wall and in it a small door shaped in the traditional keyhole curve. Raoul took a key from a small concealed niche low in the wall and inserted it in the lock. The door swung in soundlessly and he motioned her through.

After a hesitation she complied, standing like a small tremulous wraith in the darkness while he closed the door behind them. He did not immediately move to her side, and a moment later she knew why as a soft amber radiance glowed to life and played over his dark chiselled features.

On each side of the door hung two old-fashioned coach lamps, and it was these which Raoul had lit. She saw the rose trellises, the rustic seat and crazy paving, and smelled the scents of an English country garden at dusk. Roses, lavender, meadowsweet ... so potent as to bring a rush of nostalgia. She must have sighed or exclaimed, for he spoke at her shoulder, and there was a ring of irony in his voice:

'You are surprised to discover a small corner of your native land hidden in the domain of a barbarian?'

'No!' The low-voiced protest was involuntary. She turned away, pride struggling with shame, knowing his apology deserved her own in return. 'You must understand. In moments of stress it is easy to say things one doesn't mean, and later regrets. But sometimes it is the only defence.'

'For a woman—yes.' He moved slightly and leaves rustled softly in the darkness. 'But a woman has no need of the weapon of vituperation. Do you not know, Melissa, that woman's supreme strength lies in her weakness?'

She was silent, and it felt like weakness.

He said, 'It is her strongest weapon, and her greatest defence, if she chooses to use it that way.'

'Then it's failed for me, obviously.'

'Has it?'

His hands closed over her shoulders and the warm hard strength of him drew her back against him like a magnet. Melissa trembled. The spell of the enchanter coursed through her veins like wildfire, this enchanter whose magnetism she had sensed at the very first moment of meeting. But not until this moment had she comprehended the extent of the force latent within herself; a treacherous force that fired every sense with the urge to respond to that dangerous magnetism.

She knew he was going to turn her within his arms, that she was going to be powerless to resist, that her mouth wanted to experience the seeking power of those firm arrogant lips already parted to claim ... She tried to make her limbs obey her, and she did not know now which she feared most—the man, or herself. Then she saw the thin glint of gold as he moved, and with fierce desperation she grasped at the small gold object that swung from a fine chain within the open neck of his shirt.

'Is this a medal?' she said wildly, uncaring of its possible significance or that her action might seem stupid. 'They—they're quite fashionable for men these days.'

He remained quite immobile, his hands still on her shoulders, and looked down at her. 'Not exactly. It's an amulet.'

Her feverish fingers now told her that the broken shape was not that of a disc. She peered at it, half seeing, half sensing the wishbone shape and the little curved bars crossing it.

'Are you superstitious?' he asked.

'Sometimes.' She let the amulet fall and it settled back against his skin and slid within the folds of his shirt. 'It's rather super,' she took a step back, wishing her heart would settle down a bit more, and managed a tremulous smile, 'and very unusual.'

'You think it an attractive bauble?' A strange smile

touched his mouth.

'Mm,' she felt relief that the situation seemed to be getting under her control again, 'I hope it brings you luck.'

'It will.'

He had released her. His hands went to his neck and the next moment the chain was being slipped lightly over her head. The small gold weight came to rest between her breasts, and Raoul said lightly: 'Now it will bring you luck.'

'Me? But...' Her fingers sought the amulet and she stared wildly at him. 'But you can't mean ... no ... I didn't mean...'

'But yes.' He checked her instinctive attempt to remove it. 'It is yours now—perhaps you are more in need of its properties than I.'

'Oh no! I can't take it. It—I...'

'You must. It is the custom. You are my guest, and therefore whatever I possess must be yours if you desire it.'

The strange little smile came again as he regarded her startled face. 'I'm sure you do not wish to break our custom, which is a genuine one, I assure you, throughout our land. If a guest should admire any possession of his host then that possession is given, with wholehearted sincerity. You will offend if you refuse such a gift.'

She gave a gasp of dismay, and the stammered protests died on her lips. How did she deal with this fresh shock? She couldn't possibly accept such a gift, one almost certainly of gold and of great intrinsic value. Yet it seemed she couldn't return it. How to plead that she had been ignorant of the custom, without...?

Raoul was the most unpredictable man she'd ever met, not to say the most alarming. She opened her lips, and he raised a warning hand.

'No, Melissa, do not be angry again. The night has veiled those sparks in your eyes and softened that fierce independence of your mouth. I much prefer to see you thus.'

Suddenly she was aware of feeling small beside him, of the sense of male power overwhelmingly disturbing. The soft breeze feathered through her hair and then stilled into the breathless silence.

He said softly: 'The night has revealed your beauty, and made you desirable.'

His arms drew her effortlessly into the spell of enchantment. Tawny stars glittered in his eyes, then went dark as his mouth came down to hers. The long lean strength of his body was hard against her, an invading force that became a conquest of soft contours striving to remain remote. The touch of his lips was sweeter than she could ever have believed, even when his arms tightened convulsively and the sweetness became a passion without mercy. Suddenly it was as though she inflamed him, and his fire would consume all her strength of resistance.

Abruptly, his mouth slid to her cheek and his breath quickened against her flushed face. She was trembling so much she could not move, even though her whirling senses told her to break free. For this delirious moment she didn't want to be free. She wanted to entwine her arms about him and return to the fierce claim of his mouth.

His hands moved over her shoulders and he said roughly, the words forming against her lips: 'Are you

114

still my enemy, Melissa?'

'I—I was never your enemy,' she whispered shakily.

He drew back slightly. 'Even though I invoked such anger in you?'

The veil of her lashes drooped. 'One can anger without bearing enmity.'

'So I have always believed. I am glad.' He put his hand under her chin and forced her to look up. 'You see, submission is quite easy after all. And much sweeter!'

'Oh no!' She started back as though he had struck her, and stared at the light of triumph in his eyes. With an effort she gathered back composure and managed to laugh scornfully. 'That wasn't submission, my dear Raoul.'

'And what was it?' he said in a voice that had gone dangerously quiet.

'You can call it submission,' she flashed. '*We*, if we bothered to define it, would call it flirting. It can,' she said over her shoulder as she turned away, 'be just as sweet as—submission.'

CHAPTER VI

IN all fairness to Raoul she had to admit during the next few days that he wasn't quite as ruthless a gaoler as she had first believed. Perhaps he had realised that to keep three girls isolated at Kadir was to risk a quarrelsome and unpleasant atmosphere, if not an explosive one, but whatever it was he made sure the next few days were fully mapped out. The little place in the hills to which Amorel had referred proved to be a small new hotel set amid the rich picturesque scenery of the High Atlas.

They drove out in the morning, winding a leisurely exploring way, and returned long after sundown and the call of the muezzin from the minaret of the little walled town of Kadir. The following day he took them to the plantation where smiling girls brought them the traditional gift of plump dates on long heavily laden stems, and later he took them to explore Kadir. The esteem with which Raoul was held soon became very obvious. The Amghar, or El Kadir, as some called him, was certainly both respected and loved, and because of this so were the three girls.

But Melissa, in spite of this freedom, had cause for concern on more than one count. She was conscious always of the solid if quiet presence of Mahmoud and the dark-skinned chauffeur whom she remembered from that first day in Casa. If one of the girls turned away, caught by something that attracted a tourist eye, one of the burly shadows or Raoul himself was always there, vigilant, and Melissa knew that the threat was still foremost in his mind. By the weekend, with which they rounded off the week by spending it in Marrakech at the home of one of Raoul's friends, she was used to the shadows of a bodyguard. But she was far from resigned to the presence of Raoul himself.

Since that disturbing episode in the garden she had known many moments of anguish. Certain remarks returned constantly to haunt her, bitterest of all the arrogant assumption: *'If I desire a woman's submission I do not have to browbeat her into it—there are more pleasurable ways . . .'* How easily he had proved the proud boast!

The bitterness of the memory helped to stiffen her resolve to maintain a cool, hostile front in his presence. But in spite of this the damage had been done. She could don an aloof, impersonal politeness, but she could not subdue the tumult of her traitorous senses. Even the slightest of accidental physical contact was sufficient to bring those senses to tingling life, and even to look at that lean chiselled mouth, catch the regard of those dark compelling eyes, brought a potency of memory almost unbearable.

It was inevitable that Avril's sharp eyes would notice and speculate.

'What's the matter with you?' she asked suddenly, the day after they returned from Marrakech and began to gloat over the results of their shopping orgy.

'Nothing,' said Melissa.

'Oh yeah! You've been like a wet week ever since you got here.' A cynical little smile twitched Avril's mouth. 'I suppose you've discovered that Raoul doesn't think much of English girls.'

'I couldn't care less what sort of girls he likes,' Melissa said stubbornly. To try to change the subject she turned to Amorel, in whose room they were at that moment, and touched the delicately embroidered blouse the younger girl was trying on. Amorel had gone gay, buying a full traditional costume of *serwal* and filmy blouse, a caftan of sumptuous white brocade and silver threadwork, and the cloak-like *mansouriah* which completed the ensemble.

It was this last garment which attracted the girls most of all, with its distinctive patterned bands of turquoise in the misty, almost transparent tissue-like silk.

'Isn't it romantic?' Amorel crooned, preening in front of the mirror. 'Wait till Larry sees me in this.'

'He'll devour you,' observed Avril, 'if Raoul doesn't do so first.'

'No.' Some of the elation faded from Amorel's face. 'You are right. He does not really approve of English girls.'

'I wonder why,' said Avril carelessly. 'It must be my sister's fiery temper.'

'No, it is not that.' Amorel took off the *mansouriah* and sat down on the bed. 'It is because of his mother.'

Melissa looked up sharply, but left it to her sister to make the obvious prompting.

'His mother was English. He doesn't like to talk about it. She left here and went back to England when Raoul was only a small boy.'

'You mean she just walked out on her husband and the kid?'

Amorel nodded. 'I believe there was another man,

118

an Englishman she'd known when she was younger. My Uncle Pierre—Raoul's father—did everything to get her back but without success. He idolised her. Then he had an accident two or three years later while he was out riding. He lay in the desert with a broken leg. By the time they found him it was too late.'

'Heavens! Poor old Raoul. He did have a rough time of it.' Avril sounded concerned enough, but Melissa suspected the concern was somewhat superficial. The next moment she knew she had not misjudged the sister she knew too well.

'Somebody should try to make it up to him.' The flippancy was back in Avril's tone. 'Obviously he needs a woman's tender influence. I told you you ought to try being nice to him, Lissa. Just think of all that frustrated need for mother love locked up in that poor little boy. Growing up with all his illusions of womanhood shattered. That sort of thing's just up your street, Lissa. Lame ducks and lost children.' She turned to Amorel. 'She's always been first with the banner-bearing for deserving causes.'

'Shut up!'

With a furious glare at her sister's unrepentant grin Melissa walked out. Back in her own room she stared at the peaceful *riad* with brooding eyes. This unexpected glimpse into Raoul's background came as something of a shock, even though when she reflected on it she was not surprised as much as disturbed. From the start she had sensed an indefinable difference in Raoul. Compared to Philippe he was not wholly French, nor was he English, and he certainly didn't fit completely into the Moroccan pattern of nationality, despite the fact that he was utterly and perfectly at

119

home in what he proudly called his native land.

She sighed; now she knew the reason for the small secluded garden hidden within high walls which was so English and so puzzling. A husband who idolised his foreign bride might well have tried to import a touch of her native soil . . .

But now she came to look back, a certain deeper significance suddenly leapt to mind. There had been a deliberacy in the way Raoul had taken her into the intimacy of that hidden garden, and there proceeded to teach her submission.

How much of that earlier disillusion prompted his action, and the choice of scene in which to play it? Did he really despise English girls?

From the dressing-table drawer she took the amulet which had lain there ever since the night she wrenched it off and flung it angrily out of her sight. For the first time she examined it closely. There was no doubt that it was gold, as was the chain on which it hung, and that it was of considerable age. There was a smoothness at the edges and a slight blurring of the fine engraving from the years of contact with his bronzed skin as it lay against his heart.

She weighed it in her hand, the faint frown persisting in her troubled eyes. Why had he given it to her? It didn't fit in with Avril's surmise. If you despised a person you didn't present them with a personal possession of unique worth, and the more she thought about the amulet the more her conviction increased that it did hold a personal value for Raoul. So why?

Almost without volition, she raised her hands and slipped the chain over her head. The small cool weight of the amulet slid to its nadir and at that moment a shadow fell across the open window. She looked up at the tall figure and could not restrain a gasp.

'I beg your pardon, I didn't mean to startle you.' His tone was chill, and so were the eyes that instantly took in the amulet she had donned. But he made no comment, brushing aside her confused disavowal.

'There is someone to see you.'

'Me?'

'Come, is it so surprising? I should have known you would deliberately flout my wishes.'

'But I don't understand!' She stared at his angry face. 'I haven't flouted your wishes. There must be some mistake.'

'There is no mistake.' He turned away with an arrogant gesture of dismissal. 'Go and see for yourself. You will find your visitor in my study.'

Still staring her puzzlement, she went slowly past him and along the terrace. At the open screens she halted, blinking into the shadows that seemed so dark after the brilliance of the sun, and the man within swung round quickly at her entrance. He threw out his hands and rushed forward.

'*Mon ami!* At last I find you,' cried Philippe St Clair.

* * *

'Well, Philippe, I award you full marks for detection. You're brilliant!'

Philippe bowed an acknowledgement of Avril's mocking compliment and murmured deprecatingly: 'It was so simple I do not know why I didn't think of it sooner.'

They were gathered in the *riad*. The evening meal was over and Philippe was obviously enjoying basking in the smiles of three attractive girls.

'How long can you stay?' asked Amorel.

'Ahem ... I do not wish to impose on the hospitality of Monsieur Germont, and I have only a few days of vacation due at present.' Philippe's head tilted to one side and he regarded Amorel with the whimsical expression that Melissa found oddly endearing.

He's much younger than I realised back in Casa, she reflected, content to sit back while he chattered to the two girls. Beside Raoul his boyishness had been sharply accentuated.

And yet he had gone to a great deal of trouble to trace her, and after a not inconsiderable journey had been prepared to challenge Raoul Germont to deny that the two sisters were under his roof.

'I wish I'd seen his face when you turned up at the gate demanding admittance,' Avril was saying. 'What did he say?'

Philippe shrugged. 'After his first surprise at seeing me I got the impression somehow that he was not in the least surprised, after all.'

A trace of bitterness crossed Melissa's face. She knew very well the cause of Raoul's lack of surprise— and his anger. She would never convince him that she hadn't informed Philippe of her whereabouts, or that Philippe had not even received her letter, which was doubtless still lying at his office, waiting his return to Casa. Philippe, after discovering she had not returned to the hotel, had made enquiries of the reception clerk and what he had learned had made him instantly suspicious. It had not taken him long to discover the identity of the owner of the house with the amulets, and from there was but a step to the Kadir estate and the date plantations which Raoul Germont had inherited from his grandfather. It was the only lead, and Philippe had backed his hunch, taken a few days leave and set off for Kadir. Given contacts in the business world of Casa and more knowledge of the country, Melissa might have made the same discovery herself and so traced Avril.

He made it all seem so simple, she thought. No wonder Raoul was furious under that cool urbane outer appearance. He might have known he couldn't hope to keep their presence a secret. There was a sense of satisfaction running through her as she mused on Philippe's astuteness, and at that moment it did not occur to her that there could be a sinister significance in the fact of the ease with which Philippe had succeeded in discovering Kadir.

He stayed for three days and his effect on Avril was predictable. Her air of boredom dropped away like magic and she monopolised his company with blatant determination, to the extent of disappearing with him for the best part of a whole day. The night before his departure they went to dine at the Caravanserai.

Feeling uncomfortably like a proverbial gooseberry, Melissa did not enjoy the evening and she could not subdue a feeling of hurt at the marked contrast in Raoul's attitude to herself as against that to his cousin. The protective air he always had for Amorel seemed more marked that night, but his politeness to Melissa was the iciest she had ever experienced. He seemed determined to hold her responsible for Philippe's advent, and it did not make the situation any happier when Amorel said teasingly: 'I thought Philippe came to find you.'

She passed it off with a shrug, aware of Raoul's sardonic gaze.

He said, 'The best laid plans . . . Miss Blair?'

The reversion to formality carried a sting she was unprepared for, and Amorel gave him a sharp look. 'You've gone formal, all of a sudden.'

'I suspect Miss Blair prefers my formality.'

Amorel sighed as though she was aware of the underlying tension. She twisted the stem of her wine glass between her fingers and stared across the lamplit terrace where the figures of Avril and Philippe were faintly luminous against the silhouettes of the palms. They were standing very close together and Avril had her hands resting against the lapels of Philippe's white dinner jacket as she looked up into his eyes. It was a gesture as old as Eve and it brought another sigh from Amorel.

She said wistfully, 'Just look at those stars and that sky. If only . . . It's not fair!'

Melissa knew exactly what she meant. It was the kind of night and the kind of setting for sharing, and not with another girl who was experiencing the same restless, instinctive sense of longing.

She glanced at Raoul, then wished she hadn't. He was leaning back, tendrils of filmy blue rising from the cheroot he held, and his eyes were studying her as though they discerned every hidden nuance of her unease. Although he had not moved by as much as a flicker she felt his nearness and the throbbing senses start up again. As though she were back in time she could feel his hands, his mouth . . . It took a conscious effort to break free of his gaze and turn abruptly to look across the terrace. Avril and Philippe had disappeared, doubtless to explore the beautifully laid out garden of the Caravanserai, and suddenly a wave of bitterness surged over Melissa. Her sister really was the limit. She hadn't even the decency to return to the table and be sociable. After all, Raoul was their host, and she was his employee.

She started as he spoke.

'It isn't real, you know.'

'What isn't?' asked Amorel.

He smiled at the dreaminess still patent in her eyes. 'The magical air of romance that is arousing such frustrated envy in your hearts.'

Melissa noticed the plural. She said coldly, 'I hadn't noticed it.'

It was a feeble response, and she knew it.

'No, because the main ingredient is missing. I'm sorry,' he said smoothly, 'I do not care to see two such unhappy faces, but what can I do? I cannot take you both out into that moonlight and murmur the endearments I'm quite sure Philippe is murmuring at this moment.'

For a moment Amorel stared at his lean, mocking features and she seemed to be hovering between laughter and tears. The first might have won, had not Raoul added, 'And I'm sure it's not from me you want to hear them.'

Amorel's mouth twisted. 'Raoul, you're a beast! You've a heart of stone. You make it all seem horrible and——and not true.'

'It isn't true. That is what I'm trying to tell you. Why is it that a woman can be so easily blinded by the trappings of love? She must have the artifices, the assurances, she must don her artifices of dress and glamour, then she is ready to play her part in the meaningless pleasantries of flirtation. Why?'

'Because that's how we find out about each other,' said Amorel sadly. 'It's part of falling in love, and the trappings, as you call them, are not artifices at all; they're defence, until we find out the reality behind them.'

'So that you hide your heart?' The question was directed at Amorel, but the accompanying glance strayed to the silent Melissa. 'The more I think of it the more I'm convinced that you make it a game.'

'That's the way we play it.'

'Experiment, you mean. You have become very English in your outlook, *ma petite*.'

'And you've become very autocratic.' Amorel was beginning to look decidedly fed-up. 'You're about as romantic as—as . . .' a suitable epithet eluded her and she ended with a sigh of exasperation while Raoul burst out laughing.

'What's the joke?'

Avril and Philippe arrived and looked curiously at the trio. No one chose to respond, and Avril sank gracefully on to one of the little scarlet-cushioned white chairs. 'It's a heavenly night. It's a shame to leave it.'

'Why should we?' Philippe's eyes seemed to convey a secret.

But Avril gave a small shake of her head and by tacit consent the party prepared to return to Kadir. It was a silent two-hour journey through the silver-spangled night and no one seemed inclined to linger for small talk when they reached the house. Amorel went off to her room with only the briefest of goodnights and Melissa, aware of feeling in much the same mood as the younger girl, did the same.

She showered and donned a wrap, then stood uncertainly by the edge of the bed. The lassitude she had felt during the drive back had vanished and she felt so wide-awake she knew she would never sleep. Stillness had descended on the house and a sense of unutterable loneliness pervaded her spirit. Restlessly she wandered out on the terrace and leaned against the open grille.

She had felt so delighted when Philippe arrived out of the blue; and how quickly that delight had dissipated. Now she knew indifference to his departure tomorrow. If she never met Philippe again it wouldn't matter. All she wanted at the moment was to turn her back on them all, Avril included, and return to normality. And by this time next week she should be back. The day of Amorel's birthday was very near. Once it was over the need for her sister's presence here would be over as well, and so would her own enforced stay.

Melissa straightened, about to move back into her room, then stiffened as a whisper of voices came to her hearing. Along the terrace two shadows moved into view under the faint spill of lamplight from one of the other windows.

Melissa's first impulse was to move quickly, but awkwardness and the instinctive wish not to be seen kept her motionless. Her expression dispassionate she waited for Avril and Philippe to move on and continue their extended farewells in privacy. She could see the misty folds of Avril's gauzy stole and hear the murmurs of her voice, although she could not distinguish what Avril was saying. Then Avril moved towards the garden and half turned towards her companion holding out her hands as though pleading for something, and Melissa recognised her companion. It was not Philippe, it was Raoul.

He said something, and Melissa got the impression of an argument in progress, then Avril laughed softly, the note of triumph quite discernible, and swayed forward. The two shadows merged into one, stayed one, and a quivering sigh escaped Melissa.

Uncaring whether she betrayed her presence or not, she ran into her room and drew the grille closed with an agitated movement. She flung off her wrap and scrambled into bed, and the soft rays of the lamp caught her small trembling mouth as she fumbled for the switch.

She lay stiff and straight and stared up into the darkness. At that moment she hated the whole world, and most of all she hated her own sister and Raoul Germont.

*　　　*　　　*

The sense of depression lay on her like a dull cloud when she awakened the following morning. Full wakefulness came and brought memory to life, and she turned over, nuzzling her face into the pillow. She lay like that for a long time, trying to overcome her reluctance to make the first move towards facing the new day.

Presently she stirred and reached out instinctively

for her watch, only to check the movement and swear impatiently under her breath. The first thing she was going to do when she got back to sanity was to buy a new watch. Sanity! Well, she'd been the idiot all along, hadn't she? Chasing after a sister who could manage her own life to her own complete satisfaction if to no one else's, landing herself here in a place which, while undoubtedly out of this world, in essentials was a prison—if she had made any further efforts to leave would Raoul have stopped her?—and letting its infuriating owner get under her skin ... Would he have stopped her ...? It was a question she did not care to reflect on, nor did she care to reflect too deeply on Raoul Germont himself. It aroused altogether too intense a turmoil of resentment; it also made her feel so miserable she wanted to throw things ...

She sat up jerkily and flung back the covers. A few days would soon pass, and she would never set foot in Morocco again! There wasn't even any morning tea today! She was padding back from the bathroom when the tea in question arrived, brought by, of all people, an Avril who looked remarkably and uncharacteristically full of *joie de vivre* for that time of morning.

Melissa responded to the blithe greeting with an equally uncharacteristic dourness and Avril grinned at her. 'Cheer up.'

'Bring me a bucket of sand and I'll sing you the Desert Song.' A snag in her stocking spread into a hole and she swore violently as she yanked it off again. 'What's making you so chirrupy this morning?' she added grumpily.

'I don't think you're in the right frame to hear that.

Hang on—drink your tea while I fetch you a new pair.'

Avril pranced off and Melissa stared wide-eyed at the door. Avril being helpful! She reached for the tea and wondered if her sister was feeling quite well. But after her little fling with Philippe she was bound to be feeling restored to power, especially after rounding off the night with a little romantic dalliance in the moonlight with Raoul. And much good may it do her! Melissa grumbled to herself.

She was somewhat taken aback when Avril returned and handed over a pair of nylons and also the sheerest most cobwebby tights Melissa had seen.

'Take them. I've enough to see me through till I get back,' said Avril carelessly, waving away Melissa's astonished thanks.

Melissa tucked the cobwebs carefully back into their gold envelope and looked up into her sister's face. There was something behind that nonchalance and the trace of intentness was becoming more apparent. 'What do you want?' she asked suspiciously.

'Nothing really, except...' Avril sat down on the bed. 'You did arrange with Raoul to stay until Amorel's birthday was over, didn't you?'

'Arrange isn't quite the word,' Melissa said dryly, 'but that was the general idea Raoul managed to put over.'

Avril grinned at the note of irony. 'Past history. It's all over bar the shouting—don't know what he made all the fuss about. Still, it's been worth it.'

'Has it?'

Avril decided to let this pass. 'I want you to do me a favour, Lissa.'

'I thought you did.' Melissa stood up and crossed to the mirror. Through it she watched Avril's expression flicker with uncertainty. 'Go on.'

'I want to go back to Casa with Philippe this morning. We talked about it yesterday. It was his idea. And he wants me to have my job back with him. They're going to open a bigger branch—in Rabat—and Philippe will be taking it over. Isn't it super? He says we'll be meeting all sorts of important people and entertaining the top set. It's a super opportunity ...'

'Just a minute.' Melissa continued to brush her hair. 'You haven't finished this job yet. And what about your cruise?'

Avril made a face at the sarcastic tone of her sister's query, then shrugged. 'I can always have that later. Would you mind, Lissa, if I hopped today?'

Melissa swung round and gave a sigh of exasperation. 'You know perfectly well that you'll go, whatever I say, so why ask? But you can't.' A trace of satisfaction crept into her tone. 'Hadn't you better ask Raoul first?'

'Oh, I have!'

Melissa started. The small sense of satisfaction was shortlived. 'And he said yes?'

'Like a lamb.'

Lamblike! Raoul! Melissa turned back to her brushing. 'I'm delighted to hear it. Congratulations! I'd better start packing.'

'Oh no. You can't. That's just ...'

'Can't? If you're going back with Philippe this morning I'm going to be in that car as well.'

Avril shut her eyes tight and shook her head. 'I knew you'd say that. Please, Lissa, don't be difficult.

You see, that was Raoul's condition. He said I could go, provided that you would stay with Amorel until Monday. After that he's taking her back to Casa, and you as well, naturally.' Avril paused. 'I said you would.'

'You said I . . . You've got a nerve!'

'But you've nothing to rush back for. It's only for a few days.'

'If it's only for a few days why can't you stay yourself?'

'I've just told you. Anyway, it's pointless for both of us to stay now.' Avril gestured. 'It's only for Amorel's sake, to keep her company. You needn't worry about that other business. That was our idea, you know, just after we met, and we sold it to Raoul.'

'Changing identities, you mean?' Melissa reflected that her sister was being unusually expansive.

'Mm, it seemed a lark, with our names sounding a bit alike if you say them quickly. Raoul looked down his nose at first, then a couple of days later he asked me if I was serious, would I go through with it for a few weeks and keep it a secret, not even tell Sonia, and he would . . .'

'Sonia? Is that . . .?'

'An American, she spends half the year here. I got to know her somewhere, I forget where, and I met Amorel at her place a couple of days after Amorel flew over. She's a very old friend of Raoul's.'

'Sonia is?'

'A very close friend.' Avril's eyes caught the flicker of Melissa's expression. 'You'd like her.'

'Would I?' Melissa sat down rather suddenly. 'Well, the answer's no. If you leave I leave. I don't see why I should finish off your job for you while you go off on the razzle with Philippe.'

'Jealous?'

'Of you and Philippe? Not in the least. It's the principle of the thing, after all I . . .' Melissa drew a deep breath. 'No.'

Avril grimaced. 'Raoul said you'd refuse. Oh, have a heart. All my persuasion gone to waste.'

'What did you expect it to do?'

'I'm not sure.' Avril grinned, as though at a sudden flash of memory. 'I don't know what Raoul expected last night. I think he concluded I was inviting him to seduce me. You know, that man definitely has hidden talent. But he didn't seem to take me seriously.'

'What *are* you talking about?' Melissa turned her head sharply.

'Raoul, last night. When I asked him if he'd let me off the last few days.'

'Last night . . . In the garden,' Melissa said slowly. 'That was what . . .?'

'Did you see?' Avril giggled. 'Anyway, it worked. Like a charm. You should always try charm before temper, my dear little sister. You'd be surprised how it works. With men, of course.'

'No doubt. You never waste it on women, though, do you?' Nevertheless, some of the tartness had ebbed out of Melissa's tone. Her face grew thoughtful; certain things—one thing, at least—were coming clearer, and she could not help thinking that she might have seen Raoul in a totally different light had her sister been a little more frank a bit sooner.

While she pondered, Avril exclaimed: 'I wish you'd change your mind. Honestly, I'm sorry about all the misunderstanding at the beginning. I realise now that it must have worried you a lot to make you kick up the fuss you did. But I feel sorry for Amorel,' she added with apparent inconsequence. 'There's no one here for her, except Raoul, and I think at heart she's a bit scared of him. She's scared he's going to start ordering her life about in future, and she hasn't got a clue what's going to happen to her. She likes you.'

'But I can't do anything for her, even though I would if it were possible.'

'No, but at least she'd have someone to confide in until the business is settled next week.'

'You're very understanding, all of a sudden.' Melissa sighed, aware that the doubts and mixed loyalties Amorel was experiencing were very real.

'It suits me to be understanding.' Avril shrugged. 'If you won't do it for me maybe you'll do it for her.'

'All right. I'll stay,' Melissa said at last, and received a joyous embrace from Avril, all smiles now that she was getting her own way.

But Melissa could not help experiencing a stab of foreboding when the farewells were said and Avril was borne away in Philippe's car. She glanced at Raoul as they turned to go indoors and to the foreboding was added a sense of depression. If she had expected him to show some sign of pleasure at her compliance she was doomed to disappointment for his expression was cool and remote as ever.

He disappeared after mid-morning coffee, leaving the two girls to amuse themselves, and shortly after this Amorel complained of a headache. She picked at her lunch, looking so wan and depressed that Melissa forgot her own lack-lustre feelings.

'Take some aspirins and lie down for a while,' she suggested.

'It's so hot and airless today,' Amorel said fretfully when she was settled in her room with the shutters closed against the fierce brassy rays of the sun.

It was extremely hot, Melissa had to admit, watching the younger girl with sympathetic eyes. She smiled. 'It'll pass off once the evening cool sets in.'

But it didn't. The following day Amorel was still pale and listless and complaining of malaise, and Melissa could not dismiss the impression that Amorel was fretting about something. Raoul, when told that morning, insisted that she rest and stay in her room, and before he departed to visit the plantation said to Melissa: 'It is the heat. I don't think there's anything wrong with her. However, if you think there is cause for alarm I'll send Mahmoud to bring the doctor.'

With that he departed and Melissa, still uneasy, returned to Amorel. He might have shown a little more concern, she thought. For all they knew Amorel might have picked up an infection.

She looked at the untouched lunch tray and then at Amorel's miserable little face. 'What's worrying you?' she asked. 'Are you sure it's just a headache?'

Amorel nodded. 'It's just that I . . . Oh, I don't know what's the matter with me. I just want Monday to be over.'

'Your birthday? What will happen then?'

'The lawyers will come. There'll be formalities and things. I have to produce evidence of identification, and then . . .' she sighed, 'we're going back to Casa. But I wish I knew what's going to happen after that. I . . .' she sighed again and turned her head away.

'You want to go back to England?'

'At the moment, yes. I'd give anything to be back. It's not that I don't like it here. It's just that I hate the idea of having to make my home here. I want to be free to go back home, or come here as I please. I don't want to have to choose one or the other.'

'Perhaps you won't have to choose.'

'That's what Avril said. But Raoul is my trustee here and he can stop me. Unless I give up my inheritance.'

'Is it so terribly important to you?'

'At first I thought it was marvellous.' Amorel sat up and brushed a wisp from her brow. 'But now I'm not so sure. If it was only for myself . . . But everybody hates the idea of Uncle Jules getting it all. He's an awful man. I've never met him, but according to all the family accounts he doesn't care about anything but himself. My grandfather helped him out of trouble time and time again when he was young. Then he married a young widow and took over her husband's business in Marseilles and within two years he was bankrupt. Grandfather set him up again, mainly because of his wife and two young children, and said it was the last time, he was disowning him. After that we never heard anything more of him, until Grandfather died and Uncle Jules came to see if there was anything for him.'

Amorel lapsed into silence and stared into space. There was nothing Melissa could say; certainly it was not for her to offer advice or attempt to sway Amorel towards any decision she might later regret. Presently Amorel stirred, and reached for a drink of water. She made a face and set down the glass after only one sip.

'It's warm,' she grumbled.

Melissa bit her lip, aware of the film of perspiration on her own skin. Suddenly she had an idea. 'Why don't you move into my room?' she asked. 'It's on the other side and it doesn't get the full force of the sun.'

'Don't you mind?'

'Not in the least. Come on.' Melissa put out her hand to steady the younger girl as she stood up. 'You'll find it much cooler.'

Soon after the transfer was made Amorel drifted into a sleep from which she did not awake till sundown. When she did wake she looked a lot better, announced that her headache had almost gone and proved it by eating her first proper meal for two days.

When she had finished she said: 'You've been awfully sweet to me. I'd better shift myself back and leave you in peace.'

Melissa shook her head. 'There's no need. Stay here until tomorrow. Then if you're okay you can move back tomorrow night.'

'Don't you mind?'

'Not in the least. I'll just take my night stuff and my wrap.' Melissa went to fetch her sponge-bag from the bathroom, and when she returned Amorel said, 'Don't bother. Just use anything of mine you need.'

Melissa looked down at the handful of things she had collected and gathered up her pyjamas. 'It's okay. I shan't need anything else—and it's only a few yards if I do. See you tomorrow.'

She had reached the door when Amorel said suddenly: 'Will you ask Raoul to come and see me?'

'Of course.'

Melissa deposited her things in the other room and

went to pass on the request. She found him in his study, sitting at the desk and intent over some papers. He looked up and his face held only enquiry as she started to speak.

He nodded. 'Very well. I'll see her presently, when I've finished this.' He waited, quite obviously expecting her to close the matter, and Melissa's intention of doing just that fled abruptly. Something about his offhand manner set all her earlier resentment of him simmering again. She did not move and he stared at her. 'Well?'

For a moment she held his cool glance, then she said bluntly: 'What are you going to do about Amorel?'

He frowned. 'In what way?'

'About her future? She's . . .' Melissa hesitated, it wasn't going to be easy to put it into words. She took a deep breath. 'I think Amorel's fretting.'

Raoul put down his pen and sat back. 'And why should she fret?'

'She's worried about her future.'

'She has no need to be. Her future is assured.' The furrow stayed between his brows. 'I'm afraid I don't understand.'

'I—I was afraid you wouldn't. Oh, please'—suddenly Melissa relaxed caution—'don't think I'm repeating a lot of things she's said, it's not like that at all, but I'm sure she's wondering about your own plans for her future, if you're going to insist on her adhering to the conditions of that will.'

'Of course I shall insist on that. I'm bound to, from respect to my grandfather's wishes.'

'So you're going to insist on her staying here?'

'This is her home now.' His gaze did not flicker and his expression showed no trace of softening. 'And she knows this. It was all made perfectly clear to her right at the start.'

'Yes, I know,' said Melissa desperately, 'but, can't you see? She's been brought up in England since she was a baby. All her friends are there, everything she's come to love, all the people she's grown up with.'

'She will come to love Kadir,' he said in the same inflexible tone, 'and there is no reason why her other family and friends should not visit her here.'

The final shred of caution flew. 'So it's true,' you *do* intend to make her stay here. Well, I think it's ghastly. Your grandfather had no right to make such a condition, and I think you're inhuman to insist on carrying it out. You're making her sell her freedom.'

'No one is making Amorel sell anything,' he said coldly. 'I presume this is what she wants to see me about. You have lost no time in wielding your influence, Miss Blair.'

'I haven't wielded anything,' she cried hotly. 'I've merely said what I think, and praise be you can't stop me from doing that.'

'I see.' He pushed the papers away and stood up. 'You obviously consider that life at Kadir wouldn't be worth living.'

'I do.'

'Too far from the coffee bars and the blare of transistor radios?' His brows went up. 'And the freedom to indulge every selfish whim of the moment. Are those the qualities on which you base your sense of values?'

'No, and if you think that of us it only shows how

little you know of Amorel's other life. She doesn't live in coffee bars and she isn't selfish. Can't you get it into your head that she's torn between two loyalties?'

'I know more about my cousin than you imagine,' he said dryly. 'It is *you* I'm talking about.'

'Is it?' She regarded him steadily and there was pain in her eyes. 'Well, I'd prefer to be left out of it. I never wanted to be in it in the first place.'

'You've already made that fact extremely clear. You've also made it clear that you've decided my cousin is in need of championship. Poor little rich girls —and ill-treated beasts of burden . . .' A cynical smile gathered on his lips as he walked to the door and held it open for her. 'Misguided or not, you seem to have found much in our land to enlist your sympathies.'

'Yes, I certainly have.' She faced him in the doorway. 'But it's better to have misguided sympathies than none at all.'

Head high, she walked coolly along the terrace. But once in her room the coolness vanished and the turbulence of emotions which he always invoked started up again. He was impossible! Did he expect everyone to obey him meekly and never ever dare to question his decisions? Submission! Her mouth set in a tight, mutinous line as she prepared for the night. At least there was one girl who had crossed his path who would not submit tamely to his will.

Melissa donned her thin silk pyjamas and tried to tell herself that she had put up a good fight in trying circumstances. Raoul hadn't left her much leeway in the ruthless way he had forced her into his plans but at least she hadn't left him in any doubt as to her personal opinion of him, even though the thought brought little consolation . . .

She was on the point of getting into bed when she remembered her book. For a moment she hesitated, aware that her wide-awake senses were not disposed towards sleep, and reached for Amorel's *mansouriah* which was lying carelessly over a chair. It would only take a minute to slip along to her own room . . .

Leaving the screens open and the bedside lamp burning, she · flitted softly along the terrace, then stopped as she saw the shadows within the room. Raoul was there, and she could hear his deep tones mingling with the soft husky voice of his cousin.

Melissa drew back and stifled a sigh of impatience. Even if she felt inclined to intrude, which she didn't, the thought of facing Raoul again filled her with reluctance. The book would have to wait.

She turned to make her way along the shadowed terrace towards the soft dim glow spilling from the room she had left, and suddenly a rush of sadness fell on her like a weight. Why was she such an idiot? If she'd had any sense she would have refused to listen to Avril's plea and insisted on leaving with her. It was all utterly ridiculous, Raoul making conditions about her staying. What right had he to enforce them? And what right had Avril to go off so airily?

Not for the first time Melissa wondered bitterly why she had ever been so crazy to stay involved. Why hadn't she told Philippe the whole story and asked him to take her back to Casa? Face it, she told herself with scorn, you dare not challenge Raoul's strength; *and you dare not trust your own emotions when he's around!* the small inward voice taunted.

She walked into the room and turned automatically

to draw the grilles shut, and it was all over before she could draw breath to scream.

Two shadows moved behind her. A choking pad was forced into her mouth and whipped tight. Dark stifling folds descended over her head, tightness pinioned her arms to her sides and clamped round her ankles, and she was dragged roughly off her feet.

The cry 'Raoul!' choked in her throat, and she was borne helplessly into darkness.

CHAPTER VII

MELISSA'S captors did their work swiftly and silently.

The tallest of the three figures carried her across the outer terrace and down the incline towards the little side door which now gaped open to the night. One of the others ran swiftly ahead while the third man followed like a small shadow, the dark shape in his hand held ready for instant attack if necessary.

But no one heard a single sound to indicate that anything untoward had happened. Near the main drive gates Mahmoud still lay senseless, blood trickling from a head-wound after the blow that had fallen from the darkness behind him, and in Amorel's room Raoul Germont was bidding his cousin goodnight before he strolled into the *riad* to light a cheroot and reflect on certain tasks which awaited him the following day . . .

Outside the walls of the house a battered old Land-Rover was parked without lights under the cover of a clump of stubby palms. The first of the three men was already in the driving seat and one of the others climbed in beside him while the tall man dumped Melissa without ceremony into the back of the vehicle and swung himself in beside her. The engine spurted into life and the vehicle gathered speed down the track that led away from the direction of Kadir and towards the desert.

Each jolt and lurch sent Melissa rolling helplessly

and thudding painfully on the vibrating metal floor. Her senses still whirled with shock and fear. It had all happened so quickly. She began to struggle frantically, twisting her head to try to shake free of the stifling folds over her head. It was some kind of a sack, the cords drawn in a slip noose that cut cruelly into the soft flesh of her arms. But her struggles only seemed to make the bonds tighter, and her heart thumped with frightening speed. The gag and the lack of air made the fear of suffocation very real, and with a sudden surge of terror she tried to drum her heels against the floor of the vehicle.

Her efforts did not go unnoticed when the Land-Rover lurched again and her feet encountered something soft. Unseen hands closed round her and hoisted her into a sitting position so that she rested in an angle against the framework of the vehicle. The hands fell away and the muffled sounds of movements ceased.

Her thin slippers, soft embroidered *babouches* bought in the bazaar at Fez, had fallen off and the warm dirty metal of the floor bruised her heels as she made another desperate plea for release. Where were they taking her? Why? What was going to happen to her? Who were they?

Waves of clamminess broke over her and sickness welled up from the pit of her stomach. Melissa sought desperately for gulps of air and suddenly slumped sideways. She slid down over the hump of the wheel chassis and went limp . . .

She had no means of knowing how long she had lain unconscious. It could have been minutes or hours before she opened her eyes and moved fitfully, and felt an illusion of blessed freedom.

144

But it was shortlived. The imprisoning sack had been removed, but that was all. Her hands and feet were still bound, and the gag was still tied firmly over her mouth.

Gradually her frightened eyes became accustomed to the darkness and faint shapes began to outline themselves. The vehicle still tore into the night, lurching and jolting over a potholed track that could have led anywhere, and the framed square of starlit night above the tailboard only suggested a limbo of wilderness and loneliness.

She turned her head and made out the darker blurred shape of a man.

He was lounging opposite her, his face in shadow, only faint twin gleams betraying his eyes watchful over her. She moved convulsively, making choked sounds against the gag, and felt despair close in again as he gave no indication of taking the slightest notice.

Hour after hour the nightmare journey continued, until the pearl flush of dawn crept across the sky. Full light came quickly, and just as Melissa felt she couldn't hold on to sanity a moment longer the Land-Rover slowed to a halt. The driver, a wiry young Arab, and the other man came round to the back of the vehicle, and began a sharp, unintelligible confab with the bearded man. Presently the bearded man turned back to her and untied her bonds. He waited while she rubbed at her cramped and chafed limbs, then reached up to lift her down.

She flinched, her parched mouth trying to work off the effects of the gag, then her croaking whisper found strength and she began to demand and protest.

The bearded man shook his head and snatched at

her arm, making it plain she was to follow. She dragged back, trying to fight, and the younger Arab came quickly, menace in his surly features. Their words and gestures were crystal clear: that it was useless for her to run, and wearily she stumbled along the narrow stony path.

She hadn't the remotest idea of where she was, except that it was in a wilderness. A high sandstone ridge sloped up at one side and on the other was desolate expanse of stone-strewn, undulating sandy waste. She looked back towards the dusty Land-Rover and saw the third man taking a *choukhara*, a large shapeless bag, from the vehicle. He caught up with them as they reached a deep cave-like cleft in the ridge. Into this her captors led her and took from the *choukhara* an assortment of strong-smelling edibles.

At least they were going to feed her; the lamb before the slaughter! she thought hysterically.

The dried meat they offered her was beyond stomaching, and the water, from a goatskin pouch, was tepid and nauseating. But thirst overcame distaste and she was forced to drink greedily. They left her for a little while and she managed to eat one of the unleavened rolls and a handful of dates. By now she had drawn the only possible conclusion for her abduction; they thought she was Amorel, and even if they understood her protests it was unlikely that they would believe her. So Raoul's fears had had a strong foundation, she thought bitterly. The kidnapping threat had been no empty one. Her heart contracted with fear as the implications began to dawn on her: what would be their reactions when they found out the truth?

A few minutes later they came back and gestured

146

towards the Land-Rover.

The journey recommenced, along the rough, featureless track, mile after mile, hour after hour in silence, while the sun rose high and made the heat unbearable. It was plain that they had no fear of her attempting to escape, for they left her free to huddle and shift to as comfortable a position as possible. Certainly a bid for freedom in this inhospitable terrain would end in a way perfectly predictable, she thought miserably.

Once they stopped, to let the engine cool and drink copiously themselves, then on again into the sunbaked wastes . . . Melissa dozed fitfully, trying to find escape in sleep, and was awakened by a shake from a hard bony hand.

She stumbled down and stared at her destination.

The sun was going down over the blood-red desert and painting the stone of the squat square building to rich rose. It looked like an old fort or desert post, now partly in ruins. She was led through a doorway in which the old door hung loose from a broken hinge and along a dark passage ankle deep in soft sand that had drifted in for years. A ray of hope sparked in her, leading to wild thoughts . . . if she got a chance to slip away from this ruin . . . get the Land-Rover started . . . follow the track . . . it must lead somewhere . . . But the spark was quickly extinguished as her captors opened a heavy door and thrust her into the gloom beyond. The door closed with a thud, a key grated in the big old-fashioned iron lock, and Melissa was alone.

*　　　*　　　*

They kept her in the small stone cell for two days, and those two days were the longest Melissa had ever experienced. The only light and ventilation came from a small barred window high in one wall. During the day the heat and dust poured in, during the night the cold seeped from the stone and curled in with the long eerie fingers of moonlight through the bars.

She saw no more of the three men who had kidnapped her and she assumed them to be hired, as was the sullen woman who brought food and a ewer of water three times each day. The woman apparently spoke no English, or if she did she professed not to understand Melissa's repeated attempts to reason with her. After the first dreadful night Melissa considered making a bid for escape. Fear added to anger was sufficient spur to drive her to physical attack. Could she overpower the woman, long enough to run beyond reach? The woman was hampered by the voluminous black *djellaba* she wore. If she could trip her, stun her with the only feasible weapon to hand—the heavy earthenware jug ... Could she bring herself to inflict injury? The thought of physical violence was repugnant to Melissa, but she had to do something. They had shown her little mercy, and how could she tell what their reaction would be when they discovered their mistake? At least she had the satisfaction of knowing that by the time they did it would be too late to do anything about it. Amorel would have reached her birthday; the terms of the will met, and Jules, if he was at the bottom of it all, couldn't do a thing. But what would happen to her?

The scorpion that scuttled from a crack in the floor early that morning drove Melissa to action. A scream in her throat, she watched the loathsome insect disappear and knew she couldn't bear it a moment longer. When the soft shuffling steps sounded outside and the fumbling began at the lock she was ready.

Holding the now torn and filthy folds of what once had been Amorel's beautiful *mansouriah*, she stood tense behind the door as it swung open. When the woman entered Melissa flung the folds over her head, gave her a violent push that sent her sprawling headlong amid the wreckage of the tray, and rushed out to freedom.

Freedom lasted for the three steps that took her full tilt into the young boy who stood outside.

He was strong and wiry, and Melissa was no match for him. After a brief struggle she was thrust back into the cell, the door crashed shut and he went to help the bewildered woman to her feet. Then he turned to Melissa, and there was only reproach in his young face.

'You should not do that,' he said calmly. 'She not hurt you. No one hurt you here.'

Melissa blinked through the hot angry tears smarting her eyes. 'You speak English! Why am I here? How dare you keep me here? You've no right. I'm English. I want to know why and how long you think you can get away with this. You . . .'

'I do not know. I only obey orders.' His eyes were dark and imperious. 'I cannot tell you anything except that you will be released unharmed in two days' time.'

'Two days! Why not now? How do I know you're telling me the truth? How do I . . .?'

He shrugged and turned away from her, helping the woman outside and closing and locking the door.

After that the woman did not return and the boy brought Melissa's next food. By then she had had time to recover from disappointment and cool down; she had also had time to think.

She waited until he had set down the tray, watching her warily all the time, then she managed a smile and said softly: 'I'm sorry if I hurt her, but I had to do it. Please stay and talk to me for a little while.'

'There is nothing to talk about,' he said with a trace of sulkiness.

'Yes, there is.' She sat down on the goatskins which were the only furnishings in her prison and reached for one of the bread rolls spread with some kind of cream cheese. The cheese was turning rancid, but by now Melissa wasn't quite so fussy. 'Is she your mother?'

'Yes. How did you know?'

'I guessed. You're like her in features.'

The boy stood near the door, plainly uneasy, but curious despite himself. He was about fifteen or so, Melissa judged, and he did not look like a hardened criminal. She said abruptly: 'Are they paying you well?'

'My mother needs money,' he said defensively.

'Don't we all?' She leaned back casually on one hand and looked down at her half eaten roll. 'They haven't paid you yet, have they?'

'They will.'

'They won't.' She pretended to yawn.

'You lie.'

'By Allah, I assure you I don't.'

'They will. Two hundred dirhams.'

'Wait and see.'

150

He looked at her with arrogance in his dark eyes and went out abruptly, closing the door with a bang.

Melissa looked at its grim heavy boards and pursed her lips. For the first time she saw a frail gleam of hope.

It was sundown before he returned.

Melissa did not waste time.

'You need the money badly, don't you?' she hazarded.

'My young brother is going blind. He has trachoma. With money I can pay for treatment to heal his eyes.'

'I'm sorry,' she said, with genuine sympathy in her voice. 'What's his name?'

'What is it to you?'

She shrugged. 'I do not like to think of a little boy going blind when there are drugs that will restore his sight. He is little, isn't he?' She made a measuring gesture with one hand.

'Yes, he is little, many years less than me.'

'Your English is very good. What's *your* name?'

'Ahmed.'

'Mine's Melissa.'

'It is not. Again you lie.'

She smiled faintly and shook her head. 'I don't tell lies, Ahmed. You think my name is Amorel, but it isn't. Amorel is still safe at the House of the Amulet at Kadir.'

The boy looked sharply at her and she nodded. 'Have you heard the name of Raoul Germont?'

'I may have heard of it,' he said after a cautious pause.

'He has Amorel in his care, and he will not allow anyone to take her away. And now it is too late. She

151

will have much money, Ahmed, more than you or I ever dreamed of. Enough to cure thousands of little boys like your brother of their trachoma. But you will see none of it.'

'I do not believe you.'

'No,' she sighed, 'why should you? You have no guarantee that I tell you the truth, any more than you have guarantee that Jules Germont and his accomplices have spoken truthfully. They may keep their promise, but I doubt it. Because they will have none of the wealth they have schemed for.'

She watched him closely, reading the shadow of doubt in the dark eyes, the thin hands restless at the frayed edge of the denim shirt that was too big over the slight shoulders. His mouth tightened and parted uncertainly, and his gaze shifted away, then returned. She stayed silent, playing with the gold chain at her throat, then abruptly tugged the amulet from where it lay hidden in the folds of her pyjama blouse. She weighed it in her hand for a moment then slipped the chain over her head.

'Ahmed . . .'

His gaze flickered to the glint of precious metal in her hand, but he did not move.

'This will prove my identity to Monsieur Raoul Germont. If you take it to him he will give you money to cure your brother's eyes.'

'He will give me to the police.'

This was more than likely, as Melissa well knew. She said slowly, 'If you help me to get away I will give you enough money to buy the drugs. They do not cost much, not as much as you believe.'

Still he stayed silent, his glance darting from her

face to the soft gleam she held. Melissa felt despair gripping her again; it was hopeless: he would not be bribed. Then there was a quick movement and Ahmed was crouching beside her.

He snatched at the amulet, stared at it, then raised eyes in which astonishment gleamed. She said, 'This in itself is worth quite a lot of dirhams, but ...' she sighed and her mouth drooped, 'I do not want to part with it.' *Though it looks as though I've had it,* she said to herself sadly.

'This is yours?'

She nodded.

'Who gave it to you?'

'Raoul Germont.'

He was tracing the shape of it, smoothing its worn surface almost reverently. Suddenly he stood up and thrust the chain over her head. 'You must not part with it ...' He broke into Arabic, shaking his head, and she stared at him in some puzzlement.

'No, I not take.' He backed away. 'I send my mother to you now, and do not hurt her, English missie.'

'No, I won't hurt her,' she said wearily.

When he had gone she sponged her face and hands in the bowl of water and tried to make herself comfortable for the long dark hours of the night. The woman did not reappear, neither did Ahmed, and Melissa huddled down on the skins and tried not to think about scorpions ...

By the following day her spirit had failed her and she felt weak and listless. The woman brought her food at sunrise and left wordlessly, and Melissa gave herself up to depression. This was her third day in this dreadful place, and a sickness of spirit as well as body brought its soul-destroying misery.

How long? Surely Jules must know by now that his scheme had failed. Supposing he went back to France? Supposing no one knew she was here? Even if Ahmed set her free how was she going to get back? She had no money. Her passport and all her clothes were at Kadir. She had nothing, no means of identification, and she had a strong suspicion that she was no longer even in the land of Morocco. Her hair was dirty and tangled, her thin pyjamas filthy, and she felt like death.

Melissa shivered as though with an ague. Would she ever see home again, Avril, her mother ...? Her head was splitting ... she felt sick ... things were crawling all over her ... the skins stank ... and she wanted Raoul Germont more than anything else in the world ... no matter how he tormented her ... she wanted him, and the sun on her face, and soft scented water over her body, silken comfort against her skin, and someone to restore order and sanity to chaos ...

In the airless heat of the afternoon she wept, and as the black shadows of the window bars stretched to long spokes across the cell she fell into the sleep of exhaustion because she could cry no more.

The black shadow crept after the spokes as they moved slowly across Melissa's small wan face. The waning sun deepened to crimson and burnished a fiery halo round her titian head. There was a commotion, angry footsteps outside, and the door swung back with a crash.

Raoul Germont stormed in and stopped. His horrified glance roamed the cell and he gasped aloud.

'*Mon Dieu!* What have they done!'

He sprang forward and dropped to his knees, and a badly frightened Ahmed shrank back in the doorway.

Melissa stirred at the urgent crying of her name. She moaned softly and reached out blindly towards the voice. It had to be a dream. But because it was a most wonderful dream she didn't want to wake up to reality. Not when it was Raoul's arms gathering her up to him, holding her head against his shoulder, touching the tear-shadows under her eyes, lifting her effortlessly up into his arms.

She whispered incoherently, burrowed her face close against his breast and gave a great shuddering sigh. In the time-span of a dream she was in his arms; in his arms she was safe from the world . . .

*   *   *

'Melissa. Will you try to wake up! You are safe now.'

She shivered, her eyes wide and dilated as she tried to believe it was true. She was huddled on the front seat of the Mercedes, and Raoul was looking down anxiously into her face.

He drew back into the starlit night outside and she started back into full consciousness. She reached out frantically. 'Don't—don't . . .'

'Don't what?'

'Don't go away,' she whispered.

'But I'm not going to go away.' His dark proud features swam back into the dim light from the dash. 'I am merely going to get something to put over you.'

'Oh.' She clasped her bare arms, remembering the scantiness of her attire and the cold of the desert night. 'I—I can't believe that it's all over.'

'Yes, it's all over. You are safe again.' There was a note in his tone that she had never heard before, a note that warmed and made her heart ache at the same time.

He had heavy folds of white over his arm, and they brushed against her as he ducked in at the open car door. 'They frightened you very badly, didn't they? But it is over now, like a bad dream. Now sit forward . . . no, do not try to get out . . . you are like a small frozen gazelle that has been lost for a long, long while . . .'

He was shaking out the folds of the heavy white *djellaba*, placing it round her shoulders, wrapping it across her as tenderly as though she were some small lost creature. In the confined space he was very near her, the strong warm hands bringing a magic contact that she didn't want to lose. The folds of the robe enveloped her and she snuggled her chin down into its softness. It smelled warm and clean, and a faint masculine fragrance lingered in its fibre. She curled her feet up under it and relaxed, giving way to an exquisite relief that was almost pain. It was all part of the dream, and she didn't want it to end, ever . . .

He closed the door on her and went round to the driving side. The engine purred into life and it sparked off the restoration to normality. It was dispersing the dream, even though she tried to watch the starry heaven above and imagine the dream going on and on up the silver streams the headlights were making through the darkness.

She said: 'Amorel ... is she all right?'

'She is perfectly safe. And she is well guarded.' His tone was quiet and reassuring. 'There is nothing to worry about now.'

She shivered. 'I hope so. It was dreadful. They ...'

'Do not talk about it just yet. I know there are many questions and answers to be made, but there will be plenty of time for that when you have recovered from your ordeal.'

She stole a glance at his profile and saw that it had settled back into the sharp-cut imperious visage she knew best of all. She sighed, too weary to try crossing his will, but there was one thing she had to know, to complete the dream ... 'Are we going to Kadir?' she asked.

'Not immediately. It is too far a journey to make tonight.'

She considered this for a moment, recalling the long hours in the racketing discomfort of the ancient Land-Rover, and knew a surge of disappointment. 'I don't care how long it takes,' she said on a sigh.

There was a silence, and she sensed him directing a brief glance towards her. 'You are so anxious to see Kadir again?'

A flicker of caution disturbed her. She said carefully, 'Kadir will be like heaven after that—that ... Where are we? Do you know?'

'We are about fifty miles into Algeria.'

She said nothing, her suspicions confirmed that her kidnappers had taken her out of Morocco. After a brief silence she said, 'Where are we going now?'

'I'm taking you to friends. Then we will continue our journey tomorrow.' He paused, then added in the

157

same cool tone: 'At this time tomorrow evening you will be back in Kadir. And this time next week you will be back in your own country. Does that thought make you feel any happier?'

There was no response. Melissa let her eyelids droop. That thought did not bring happiness, and she did not dare dwell on the secret her heart wanted to tell. *That* wouldn't bring happiness, either.

Raoul drove on into the night, the car rock steady under the strong capable hands on the wheel. Melissa stayed unmoving, curled up tight within the enveloping robe, and tried not to think about Raoul the way her heart wanted her to think about him. Presently the speed of the car slackened and she came out of her brooding to peer at the shapes of small square buildings, pale and faintly luminous in the moonlight. The car passed beneath a high curved opening in a wall and emerged into a narrow street amid the huddle of houses.

Raoul did not volunteer any information and she concluded that this must be the destination of which he had spoken. She was preparing herself to move, uncurling her stiff limbs, when to her surprise the car's speed quickened again. The castellation of roofs against the velvet blue came to an end and the open country came into view.

Almost another hour had passed before Raoul at last halted the car. The sting of the crisp desert night and the shifting sand underfoot effectively dispersed Melissa's drowsiness when she scrambled out of the car. Hugging the robe about her, she stared at the black outlines of the tents and felt little surprise. Somehow she had known it would be an encampment.

158

He touched her shoulder and she moved forward, to stumble and almost fall as her foot caught in a fold of the overlong *djellaba*. He caught her instantly, and for a moment she thought he was going to swing her up into his arms.

She gave a muffled exclamation and snatched at the robe, moving away from him. 'Which way?' she said, not looking at him.

'Here,' again he touched her, groping for her arm, 'watch that you do not stumble again.' There was a big over-lapping fold at the tent entrance. Raoul drew it aside and motioned her into the darkness. His fingers tightened momentarily on her arm. 'Wait here.'

He had taken a small flashlight from his pocket. She watched its wavering pencil of light as he moved away from her and tried not to give way to the fret of impatience while she waited for him to return. Was this the same encampment that he had visited on the never-to-be-forgotten day when she had hidden in his car? It could not be, it must be many miles away. But these people moved around all the time, following the old trade routes and spice trails across the desert. She heard voices, saw the flare of hastily lit lamps, and Raoul came back with a tall bearded man in a blue robe.

Briefly he introduced her to Shaik Yusef Ibn Haruni, and the big man inclined his head gravely, bidding her welcome.

Raoul said, 'Shaik Yusef has summoned a serving woman. She will take you to your quarters for the night and see that you have everything you require.'

'Thank you.' Suddenly she felt small and lost and unsure of herself in these strange surroundings. She could now take in the great silken drapes that formed the ceiling of the tent, and the rich rugs of brilliant hues which carpeted it. The woman came almost immediately, and afterwards it was much as Melissa remembered of the earlier occasion.

She was given refreshments; freshly made sweet mint tea, little sticks with savoury *kebabs,* sweetmeats of almond and honey and plump glistening amber dates, and after she had eaten bathing water was brought and oils to rub on her body. There were also articles of dress, soft fine cotton *serwal*—the filmy pantaloons that the outer caftan completely concealed —and an embroidered, loose-fitting blouse, but Melissa clung obstinately to the voluminous white *djellaba* before the women took her to their apartment.

There they withdrew, leaving her a lamp which they set on a low stool beside the pile of cushions on which presumably she was to sleep.

But now sleep was the last thing Melissa wanted. She sat on the camel-hair blanket and stared at the flickering shadows cast by the lamp. The division of time into day and night, and the fitting of regulated actions into those times no longer seemed important. The hour could be anything between eight and the small hours of the morning, and she had not thought to ask Raoul what time it was, but judging by the fact that the encampment had retired it must be very late. She stood up, secured the robe more securely so that it would not trip her, and wandered to the opening in the tent wall.

The night was very still, the moon swinging low, and there did not seem to be a soul abroad. She hesitated, then abruptly went back into the tent, to emerge with a cushion which she propped at the opening; she had no wish to mistake her quarters in the dimness. That risk taken care of, she paced slowly past the great dark canopies until she reached the perimeter of the encampment. A grunt nearby made her start, then laugh nervously as she made out the shapes of the resting camels. A little farther on the goats were tethered, and she moved on with the intention of completing a circle about the camp. She was half-way round when the shadow detached itself from the other shadows and Raoul confronted her.

'Why are you not resting?' he demanded in peremptory tones.

'I wanted air, and to walk.'

She began to stroll on and he fell into step at her side. 'If you wish to walk you must have an aim. We will go to the oasis, as there is no other aim.'

'Where's the oasis?'

He smiled in the darkness. 'This is the oasis, but the part which the visitor thinks of as the oasis lies this way, at the other side of the encampment.'

'Oh.' She followed his steps obediently, climbing the incline of a dune that skirted the area like a big crescent moon, until they descended into the hollow where the green began and the clusters of palms edged the water hole.

He said, 'It seems little to see at this moment, but it is the most wonderful sight to the desert traveller.'

'Yes, I should imagine it is. Raoul,' she turned her head, 'how did you find me?'

'Through the amulet. Ahmed recognised it and came to seek me.'

'I—I tried to bribe him to let me go.' She frowned,

161

wondering if she was imagining a slight restraint in him, and certain that the amulet held some significance which was still unknown to her. 'It seemed to startle him,' she said slowly, 'as though it meant something to him. He refused to take it, and I . . .'

She stopped, aware that she had made an admission she had not intended to make. She looked at him, and now she was concerned. 'I—I didn't want to—— Try to understand, Raoul. I didn't want to part with it, but I was desperate, and it was the only thing I had with me that held value.'

'I quite understand. It was natural in those circumstances, however,' he turned and moved back in the direction of the camp, 'I am glad that it was not necessary for you to part with it.'

Slowly she matched his pace, her hand going unconsciously to the charm at her throat. 'Do you want it back?' she asked uncertainly.

He paused. 'You wish to return it?'

'No, it isn't that, it's—it's just that I know it means something special, and that in some way it had something to do with your rescuing me. But if you don't want to explain it doesn't matter. Only I know it has sentimental value to you and I don't want to take it from you because of that—that silliness that night,' she ended in a rush.

'Silliness?' He stopped abruptly. 'Sentimental value?'

There was such scorn in his voice she winced. 'Well, I didn't mean it exactly like that, I . . .'

'I think you had better sit down, Melissa, and I will tell the story. It is quite a long one, and the way in which history repeats itself should appeal to your

162

romantic English mind.'

He dropped down on to the sand and rested his arm across one crooked-up knee. 'You may have noticed that some of the Berber women bear a tattooed mark on their chins?' She nodded, and he went on: 'It is the emblem of their particular tribe, deriving from the language which has become lost in as far as it is written. The amulet is in the shape of one of those symbols. Ahmed recognised it instantly. It is one used by his own tribe. Therefore tribal loyalty immediately overcame his other instincts for self-gain. He . . .'

'But he had a reason,' she interrupted. 'He wanted . . .'

Raoul gestured. 'Yes, he told me about the child and your promise. That matter is already in hand. Everything that can be done for the child will be done.'

He took cigarettes from his pocket and offered her one. When he had lit it for her he said, 'You are not cold?'

She shook her head. 'If you only knew what heaven it is to see the stars and feel free again after that ghastly stone cell!' A shiver came with the memory and Raoul gave her a curious glance.

'You feel free now?'

'Wonderfully so.'

'And Kadir no longer seems like a prison to return to?'

'A prison?' She started, unable to read his shadowy features, and memory rushed back, bringing a rush of colour which the night mercifully veiled. 'But it's different now, isn't it? I mean . . .' She gestured helplessly and looked away.

'You did not feel that way during those first days in Kadir,' he said softly. 'I wonder what has brought about that change of heart in you. Could it be that you now know from bitter experience that I did not act without cast-iron motive? Or did that English sentiment win and rouse your sympathies for my cousin?' The small scarlet tip of his cigarette described a glowing arc, then fell again. He looked down at the small averted profile and added, 'Or could there be some other reason?'

She thought she detected a note of mockery in his tone, and suddenly she was conscious again of the full disturbing power of his nearness. She said hastily, 'Of course there isn't—you were going to tell me about the amulet—and why do you keep mocking at my English sentiment? Your mother was English, wasn't she?'

'How did you know that?' His voice sharpened.

'Amorel told me.'

'I see.' There was a perceptible pause. Abruptly he buried his cigarette into the sand and stood up. 'Then you know the story?'

'Yes.' She also got to her feet, into a silence that suddenly seemed chill, and brushed the clinging sand from her robe. 'I'm sorry, Raoul,' she said sadly.

'There is no need to be.' He stood for a moment, looking down on the wide canopies sleeping under the veil of the silver moon. 'These are my people, as I am theirs. I am proud of the ties of blood and heritage.'

'The Berbers?'

'Did Amorel not tell you that part of the story?'

She stared at the hawklike profile, her eyes wide with bewilderment. 'She told me only that your mother deserted you when you were still a small child.'

'The one I think of as mother was my grandfather's beloved wife. She was a pure-blooded Berber girl, Melissa. That is the story behind the amulet.'

Apart from her now, across a chasm she could not cross, he strode down the dune towards the encampment.

CHAPTER VIII

A THIN ghostly mist hung over a blood-red desert at dawn when Raoul drove away from the encampment. There was an eerie quality in that wild alien landscape, a lifelessness that matched Melissa's subdued mood as she settled down for the long drive that lay ahead.

Raoul was uncommunicative, withdrawn into that hard shell of self-sufficiency where she could not reach him. Beyond a brief greeting, and imparting the information that it would be evening before they got back to Kadir, he had hardly acknowledged her presence this morning and she could not help a feeling of hurt.

She sighed as the car gathered speed and wondered if she had imagined his tenderness the previous day when he had set her free and taken her into his keeping, wrapping the robe about her ... She reached back into the dream, trying to recapture those nebulous moments when he burst into the cell and cradled her head in his arms. He had transformed the realm of nightmare into Elysium; but now ...

The shadows of her thoughts made a curious hardness shield the blue of her eyes; memory would not match reality, any more than would those other memories, and only the heart of a fool would attempt to make them do so, even though, for so short an acquaintance, she seemed to have far too many memories of Raoul's arms ...

Looking straight in front of her, she said, 'Will you make arrangements to take me back to Casa as soon as possible?'

'Of course. As soon as you wish. But you must be recovered from your ordeal before you make the journey.'

'I'm quite recovered now,' she returned coolly.

There was no response. She glanced sideways and saw frowning concentration on his face. It occurred to her that he was seeking some landmark and was thankful that she wasn't driving; to her untutored eye they were merely traversing a featureless waste of sand dotted every so often with patches of ilex and desert thorn, yet it never occurred to her to doubt Raoul's ability to get them safely to their destination.

After a little while the frown of intent cleared and he said suddenly: 'You're taking all this with remarkable calm.'

'I presume you know where you're going.'

'I didn't mean that—although I'm flattered by your trust.' His mouth flickered. 'I'm referring to this distressing experience you've suffered.'

'Oh, that!'

'I was expecting you to demand revenge, to flare at the fates for the indignity and the very real shock it must all have been.'

Her mouth curved bitterly. 'It's over now. It doesn't matter.'

'Oh, but it does.'

She was surprised by the vehemence in his voice. Then she remembered that it could so easily have been his cousin and the brief warmth died. 'I had three days to rage and bemoan the fates,' she said flatly. 'After a while one becomes spent. I don't feel anything now, only thankfulness that it's all over.'

'But it is not yet over. There is also the matter of Mahmoud—but of course, you will not know of that,' he interjected. 'Your assailants attacked and injured Mahmoud before they abducted you.'

'Was he badly hurt?'

'Fortunately, no. I had him taken to Casa where he is now recovering.'

'Who's looking after Amorel?' she asked, after a slight pause.

'Amorel is also back in Casa.'

Melissa turned to look at him, surprise breaking her calm. 'You sent her back alone?'

'No, with my lawyer. She is staying with Sonia.'

Melissa sank back and returned to contemplation of the scene ahead.

'She is being well cared for, but the danger is past now,' he said calmly, then shot her a brief glance. 'I could not leave Kadir until we had found *you*.'

She said nothing, aware of a coldness that could not be dispersed, even by this last statement.

He said, 'If it is any consolation, every effort is being made to find those men, and lay the blame where it originated.'

Suddenly she felt weary. None of it seemed to matter any more. Because already there was a sense of finality taking over. Soon she would be on the way back to England. Home. A pleasant bungalow on the outskirts of Odiham. She had to start looking for a job and her mother was going to ask hundreds of questions, very few of which she would dare answer with strict truth. It all seemed so far away from these hot desert skies, yet in a very short time she would be looking back on these events and they would seem far away and strangely unreal. Raoul would join Amorel and Sonia, a shadowy woman she could not visualise, who, nevertheless, was very real, and they would celebrate Amorel's good fortune. No doubt time would sort out Amorel's problems; time took care of all things in its slow but inexorable way. Avril would go her own sweet way, which for a while would concur with that of Philippe St Clair. Yes, it would all work out for them all, and the only one who had suffered . . .

'What time is it, Raoul?' she asked abruptly.

'There is a clock on the dash,' he reminded her dryly. 'Or has it stopped?'

'No.' She turned away and stared dry-eyed out of the side window.

A little while later he stopped for coffee from the flask he had filled that morning at the camp. She sipped it, staying silent and away from him. The calm she had gathered about her had been hard won; it could easily be destroyed and she was thankful when he started off again almost immediately. Then he said suddenly: 'We should reach Tell Arif within an hour.' The name meant nothing to her and he went on: 'It's a small watering place. We will eat our lunch there and stay for three or four hours until the intense heat of noon abates slightly.'

'Three or four hours!' Melissa could not check the exclamation.

'We have to cross a sand sea afterwards. You would not be able to endure the heat, apart from the effect it has on the engine.'

Her heart turned over. She knew enough of the desert and Raoul to know that whatever course he adopted was the wisest one, but the thought of several hours alone in his company made her quail. The lesser of two evils! Her smile was wry. Already it was unbearably hot and her eyes ached from the glare. Perhaps there'd be shade at the oasis, and cool water . . . The horizon was like a lake, she reflected. Shimmering waves of ochre under a sky like burning bronze. It was easy to understand how travellers hastened towards the mirage. The eyes played strange tricks, even as hers were telling her of a tall figure rising from the sand some distance ahead of the car.

She blinked. No one crossed the desert on foot, still less alone. But there was a second sand figure, rising, whirling . . . it was . . . Before she could speak the car stopped so suddenly she was thrown forward. Raoul said, 'Out—don't ask questions.'

'But . . .'

'Do as I say!' Already he was out of the car, and the hot blast of wind that lashed in effectively silenced her exclamation.

A leaping spiral of dust clouded his figure as he ran towards the back of the car. She heard the boot open, and the mad whine of the wind, and even as she fumbled for the door handle the skies were darkening. A storm was threatening, the whirling figures whipped up spirals of dust, but why on earth get out of the car's shelter?

Nevertheless, it did not occur to her to disobey. She staggered as the wind caught her, and Raoul slammed the boot lid down, turning to her with a roll of white in his arms.

170

'Get the water flasks and the *djellaba*—quickly!'

'Yes . . .' She leaned back into the car and groped for the things on the back seat. It had all happened so quickly. One moment nothing, then the peculiar hissing growl in the air, the onslaught of desert fury beleaguering them, filling her eyes with dust and stinging like a rain of hot needles on her face.

The robe billowed wildly as she emerged and she tugged the folds away from her face, struggling to close the car door. Raoul was crouching down; trying to secure the cover he had enveloped the bonnet in. She turned to try to help, and felt a resistance. A fold of the robe had caught in the door. Raoul straightened, and before she could stop it, the car door was sucked open by the force of the wind. It struck him full on the temple.

He staggered, put his hand to his head, and reeled against the side of the car.

Her cry of alarm was whipped away. She lurched towards him, grabbed his shoulder, and he straightened unsteadily, shaking his head. His lips shaped the words: 'Never mind,' and he seized her arm, urging her forward.

'Hurry!'

He half-thrust her, half-dragged her in a stumbling run. She clutched desperately at the flasks and the robe, bracing herself back against the wind that threatened to send her headlong. Half blinded by dust, she lost first one *babouche*, then the other, and hardly realised she had done so during that mad rush for the crescent-shaped crest Raoul was making for, until the burning heat of the sand struck at the soles of her bare feet.

Her breath was sobbing from her and existence centred on the hard fingers biting into her arm. It was the only thing that seemed to keep her free of an elemental force threatening to integrate her into the whirlwind of dust.

Then they were dropping down. There was a respite that was unbelievably calm, but it was a temporary illusion, she realised as Raoul made unerringly for a hollow and tried to line it with the *djellaba*.

'Down—quickly, and cover yourself.' He thrust her down as he spoke and flung himself full length beside her, drawing the folds of the robe across to shield her.

'We—we'll be buried!' she exclaimed frantically. 'We . . .'

'Keep your head down. Make the most of what shelter we have.'

'But why not stay in the car? Instead of . . .'

'It's the *irifi*—the wind from the south that we dread. It is quite likely to bury the car with us inside. Pressure could prevent our opening the doors, apart from the risk of suffocation. We are safer here.'

She subsided, her breathing beginning to steady, and then became aware of a new agitation that had nothing to do with the storm. For those breathless minutes the sand-storm's fury had driven everything else out of her mind, but now, plunged suddenly into this small haven, she came to full consciousness of Raoul's nearness, his arm still curved protectively across her body. She stirred uneasily and said raggedly: 'The flasks . . . are they . . . ?'

'They're here. Do you want a drink?'

'N-no, not yet.' She licked lips dry with sand. 'How long will it go on?'

She felt his slight shrugging movement. 'Who knows? Hours, perhaps.'

'Does that mean we have to . . .?'

'I'm afraid so.' His voice was flat, betraying no fear, and she shivered.

'Try not to be afraid.' His hand tightened with momentary reassurance on her shoulder. 'People do survive the *irifi*.'

'But what if the car is buried, and we—we can't find it?'

'Don't think about it.'

She fell silent, trying to push the dreadful thought out of her mind. The sun had vanished and the strange uniform hue hung over everything. It was as though some artist had taken his brush and varnished land and sky with a hot sullen burnt orange. The sand was invading every fold of clothing, filming the skin with that ochrous tinge, clinging and abrading, and the wind brought only fresh waves of heat to a body that already burned unbearably. Suddenly her breath caught in her throat. The storm centre of heat lay in Raoul's touch on her shoulder, she couldn't bear it a moment longer . . . She twisted restlessly, brushing sand-sticky tendrils of hair away from her face, and whispered: 'Please, I must have a drink.'

Instantly he moved, uncorking the flask and holding it out to her. 'Be careful,' he warned as she took it, 'do not drink more than you need. It may have to last us a long time.'

She stared at him, trying to still the quakes of unease, then took a sip and held the flask out mutely. Then, as he took it and replaced the cap, she saw the great darkening bruise against the deep tan on his temple. Instinctively her hand went out.

'Raoul—your head! There's an enormous bruise. It's swelling.' She made to take the flask of water again. 'Let me bathe it. It looks ...'

'Are you crazy? Waste precious water on a bruise! Melissa, do you not know ...'

'Just a little to cool it.' Her eyes distressed, she pleaded. 'It must ache dreadfully.'

'It doesn't.' He put the flask down behind him and turned, to meet her anxious stare. 'Don't look at me like that, Melissa.'

'Like what?' She started back.

'With that expression I have seen before.'

A dark intensity had entered his gaze and it held a disturbing quality. She shook her head, failing to understand, and he said coldly: 'It is the look you have for a stricken animal, filled with pity and misplaced sentiment.'

The hard tone stabbed at her and instinctively she took refuge in defence. 'I can see sympathy is misplaced. How else can I look at you? As though I couldn't care less?'

'Any way you like.' He took a handkerchief from his shirt pocket and wiped sand from his brow. 'As long as you remember that I am first a man and not in need of your sympathy.'

'Oh!' She recoiled as though he had lashed her. 'You're impossible! I'm sorry I said a word. And I *didn't* look at you like that. I ...'

A rain of dust eddied in a renewed onslaught of the wind and she turned her face away, almost glad of the pain it brought so that she could hide from his cold anger. The fierce gusts stilled for a moment and she brushed at her eyes, then dropped her face against the shield of her arm. A great rage against the fates suddenly welled in her and she knew a childish desire to kick and beat her fists against their injustice. Why? She hadn't asked to be brought here. She hadn't wanted to come to Kadir. Raoul Germont had made her come here. All that she had been through during the past few days was *his* fault! She'd tried to fight him and he'd used the most unfair tactics of all; a strength she couldn't combat and the advantage of her own worst weakness. He'd deliberately made love to her that night in the garden and made her aware of him as a lover. For a few moments of gratification of sheer male egotism. And now she was stuck in a sandstorm with him, and all he could do was taunt her. If only she could erase every memory of him, and her own foolish weakness . . .

'Why are you weeping?'

She shuddered at the sound of his voice. 'I'm not.'

'You are.' Rock-hard fingers grasped her chin and forced her to look up. Unfathomable eyes glinted down at her tear-stained face. 'You are afraid?'

She jerked free. 'No! I—I've got sand in my eyes.'

'I've sand in mine, but it does not make me weep.'

'No, it wouldn't,' she mumbled bitterly.

There was a short silence, then he leaned over her and thrust a handkerchief into her hand. 'I think we'd better remove that sand from your eyes. It is clouding more than your vision, Melissa.'

'Is it?' she flared. 'That's something you'll never understand.'

'What will I never understand?'

'How people really feel. Because you can't see further than your own narrow way. *Your* way. Never anyone else's. Only how you think people should be. You're so hard and arrogant you won't give people credit for feelings you've never experienced yourself.'

'Go on, Melissa,' he said after a pause. 'What are these creditable feelings which I don't possess?'

'Pity and compassion for other people's hopes and fears, and sufferings. People suffer as well as animals.' She stared at him fiercely and her hands clenched into small fists. 'You've despised me right from the start. Yes you have,' she cried as he made a sharp gesture. 'Ever since that day I took pity on that poor little brute in Casa you've treated me as though I were stupid and silly. Sentimental! Well, I *am* sentimental!'

She drew in a deep breath and turned away. 'That's the way I'm made and I'm proud of it. I don't want to be different and I don't care *what* you think of me,' she ended defiantly.

'But I think you do.'

'I don't, and—and I hope your head *does* ache! And I want to get out of here—and . . .'

'Don't be a little idiot!' Like lightning he forestalled her blind bid for escape. 'Don't add foolhardiness to all those other failings. Yes, *you* listed them, not I.'

His hands gripped her shoulders, kept her a trembling defiant prisoner in his hold. 'I would not have called you silly and stupid, but you *are* proud and stubborn, with the temper of a little desert cat. Will nothing tame that fierce independence?'

There was a flare of white now at the hard chiselled outline of his mouth and a muscle twitched in the lean jaw. He stared down into her transfixed gaze with eyes so intense she thought she must drown in their tawny depths. Then his arms fastened round her with the strength of coiled steel and his mouth descended to make its fierce claim.

The touch of his mouth was like fire. For a moment it consumed her, then she summoned the resistance of despair and fought to free herself.

'No!' She arched back over the coils of steel and turned her head despairingly. 'That's all you want from your women, isn't it? Physical submission. Well, you won't get it from me!'

She thrust her hands against his chest and felt the indrawn breath under the power of him. He held her without effort, and the tears of rage sparkled in her eyes. His mouth curved with amusement. 'You see, you are utterly feminine after all, my hot-headed little English miss. I think you have sand in your heart now.'

'You can say that. But at least I have a heart,' she spat. 'I don't think you have. Let me go!'

'Not till I'm ready. No, my fiery little copper-head. I must prove that I possess a heart, and I must prove something else to which you seem blind.'

'You don't have to prove anything to me that I don't know.' She was shaking, fighting a weakness that crept insidiously through her limbs. 'And your own pride should shame you. Or are you proud of the physical strength that enables you to beat down a woman's resistance with sheer brute force?'

She stared him out, determined not to give an inch.

The hot acrid light lent a bronze sheen to the impassioned features that might have been hewn from the desert rock, and the hard muscular chest against which her hands strained only brought awareness of how puny her slender strength. Then she felt the passionate rise of his indrawn breath and for a moment she thought those arms would snap her like the brittle stem of a storm-tossed flower.

'No, Melissa,' he gritted. 'I feel neither pride nor shame. But I have a notion to teach you to know your own heart—and disabuse you of these strange notions you hold of me. You accuse me of lacking heart. You call me barbarian. You have a strange way of appealing to a man. I wonder if ever in all your sheltered existence you have been at the mercy of a real barbarian.'

There was the tight anger of passion in him now, a wildness matched only by the tempest beating around them. The wind shrieked over the roar of her own throbbing pulses and she fought the traitorous weakness that wanted to implore him to make a haven within which she could shelter. She twisted blindly to shield her eyes and cried bitterly: 'Only a barbarian would behave as you do. As for mercy . . . I would as soon trust myself to the mercy of the desert than you!'

With a frantic effort she broke free and stumbled up towards the crest of the great ridge. Instantly the full force of the tempest caught her, spinning her helplessly in a vortex of flying dust. Blinded, spent beyond endurance, she crumpled on the seething ripples of sand. An oath was torn from Raoul's lips as he leapt up the dune. He bent over and scooped her up over

178

his arms and stumbled down to the scant shelter of the hollow. For a long moment he stared down at his burden with angry eyes, then shook his head and pressed the small face against his shoulder.

'Little fool! What are you so afraid of? Did you believe I'd ravish you against your will?'

'What do you expect me to believe?' A tired little sigh was lost against his shoulder as she kept her face stubbornly hidden.

'How little you know of a man's self-respect.' Abruptly he knelt and laid her down, to bend over her, hands pinned to the sand on either side of her. 'When I take a woman, Melissa, she must come willingly to me, wanting to belong to me with heart and soul as well as body. And then only if she loves me as completely and utterly as I love her.'

'If these are a sample of your methods you'll never find her,' she said brokenly.

'You think not?' Raoul's gaze bored down as though it would search out her very soul. 'But I *have* found her.'

'Then you'd better pray hard you get safely out of this.' With a desperate need for evasive action she brushed at her sand-coated arms and finger-combed through her disordered hair.

He did not move, nor did his gaze cease to search her face. As though she had not spoken he added, 'But I do not think she has found me—yet.'

Suddenly she dared not move and a new, uncanny stillness seemed to hang heavy in the air. It was as though even the tempest stayed its fierce breath and waited.

'Melissa, look at me.' His brown fingers curved

179

under her chin, forcing her to turn her head. 'For how long are you going to defy the fates and your own heart?'

'I—I don't know what on earth you're talking about,' she said with a gallant attempt at lightness. 'Only a fool tries to defy the fates.'

'How true!' His exclamation was derisive, a note of triumph in it challenging the indignation darkening her eyes. 'And how the fates must smile at mortals who duel with words when they might exult with love.'

His lean face was unbearably close, his mouth only the distance of a heartbeat away, and her own heartbeats pounded as though they would choke her. His warm breath was a caress of intimacy on her brow and she raised a trembling hand. 'Raoul, don't . . . unless you . . .'

'Are you still afraid of me?'

She closed her eyes to shut out the compulsion of those tawny-dark eyes. 'Should I be?' she parried in a whisper almost imperceptible in its weakness.

'How can I answer that for you?' His voice went dangerously quiet. 'Except to say I believe you are afraid of yourself.'

There was silence so potent she did not dare draw breath lest she shatter it and the last fragile tendril of defence. He said softly: 'How long before you believe?'

Her lips parted, trying to form the despairing doubt of sanity, yet no sound would leave them. His fingers slid away from her chin and there was no contact now, except the magnetic quality of that merciless gaze. He did not move.

'Come to me,' he whispered.

The spell snapped its bonds. Her choked murmur of his name was lost in the engulfing tide that swept away her resistance. The heartbeat of distance was lost, crushed within the circle of his arms, the final captivity of his embrace. He kissed her eyes, her brow, the curve of her cheek, and then, with soul-pervading sweetness, claimed her mouth. His arms, his kiss, his entire being seemed to merge with her own throbbing senses until she was lost in the wild sweet intoxication of his ardour.

When at last he drew back a little and looked down on her she was beyond stirring. She lay limp in his arms, her hair a tumbled cloud of coppery silk against his shoulder, and a sigh trembled through her. It was as though some great barrier had crumbled, as though some storm-tossed sea had thrust her far beyond its reach, where she lay spent and drained, waiting till the tempest ebbed.

From a long way away she heard his voice, strangely unreal, triumphant. 'Now do you believe?'

Her head swam. She fought and failed to dispel the headiness and the havoc, and turned her face blindly against his shoulder. 'Yes, I'll believe. Whatever you want me to believe. You've won,' she whispered on a sigh.

'Won?'

Her shoulders made a tiny shrugging movement of defeat, infinitely weary, as she whispered, 'Yes—I hope you're satisfied with your victory.'

The arms slackened. He grasped under her hair, at the nape of her neck, made her face him. He looked hard at her, and his eyes glittered.

'Victory! *Tiens!* Is that what you believe of me? Do you believe I desire every woman I meet? And lay siege to her own desire? *Tiens!*' he repeated despairingly. 'Can you not dinstinguish the real from the imitation?'

'I—I want to.' Her mouth trembled and bewilderment swam in her eyes. 'But I—I'm afraid to—of you—if you don't ...'

'Afraid to love!' With a groan he cradled her close, his fingers taut and fierce in her hair. 'How do I melt this stubborn little heart and make it hear mine?'

She stiffened, turned her head sharply, incredulity rushing over her as she met the burning intensity of his gaze. It couldn't be *that* which she saw in those eyes.

'What are you trying to say?' she whispered.

'Say? What am I saying with every part of me? Completely and utterly, as I have said to no woman until you came into my heart?'

'No other woman? You mean ... *love?*'

'I mean love. And you. And me.'

'Me?' Suddenly she was incoherent. Tremulous joy and wavering disbelief and conviction all whirling with the echoes of the words he had spoken. His features blurred, her eyes misted even as the radiance curved her mouth, and she could only look at him with her heart shining from her eyes.

'And you? Say it,' he prompted urgently. 'Say it.'

'Oh *yes* ...' His hands were smoothing her temples, cradling the contours of her face as she made the trembling admission he demanded, and now at last all doubts and pride were swept away as the floodgates of love and longing opened.

182

She stole tender arms around him, caressed the proud head, strained to match the ardour of his loving with all the response she had craved to make, until everything ceased to exist outside their heaven of ecstacy.

At last he drew back, and the dark fire of love smouldered in his eyes. 'You will marry me very soon?'

'Very soon.'

'And you will try to love Kadir and my desert?'

'I'll try, but never as much as I love you, Raoul,' she said softly.

'The way you say my name, with that funny little English lilt . . . I shall never tire of hearing you say it.' He brushed her lips with a lingering, feather-light kiss. 'We will live half of the year in Casa, in the house by the sea which has known so much happiness. The singing birds will make their music for you, and Casa is but a short flight from your own shores of home. But I will enchant you so much you will not be able to be homesick.'

'You've enchanted me already,' she murmured, 'and made me feel as though I don't know if I'm on my head or my heels.'

'That is how love should make a woman feel. Enchanted with happiness.'

She let her head lie against his shoulder and mused for a moment, trying to regain her breath. Then she remembered something. 'Who is this Sonia?' she asked suspiciously.

'Sonia?' He started slightly, then a wicked gleam entered his eyes. 'You are jealous?'

'Appallingly. You have a great deal to answer before

I'm convinced.'

'Sonia,' he said slowly, 'is a most charming and beautiful woman. You will meet her very soon and you will love her, I'm sure.'

'Will I?' Her voice was dry.

'Oh yes. I have no secrets from Sonia, and she is not in the least secretive about the fact that she recently celebrated her sixtieth birthday.'

Melissa closed her eyes and laughed softly. 'You weren't going to marry Amorel?'

'My cousin?' He frowned. 'I think you had better tell me all the rest of these odd notions you appear to have collected about me. What is this about my marrying Amorel?'

She curled closer to him. 'I'm betraying confidences, I suppose, but Amorel believed that your grandfather wished the marriage, and that you wished to honour his wish. Is that true?'

'Not in the sense my dramatically-minded little cousin seems to have believed. It is true; a marriage between us would have delighted him, but only if it was a true love match. He was not in the least a ruthless, dominating person.'

Melissa was silent for a moment, then took joy in her new ability to confide in him. 'You're not going to force Amorel to stay if she's unhappy, are you—darling?' she added softly.

His lips caressed her brow. 'Do you believe I would?'

'I don't know. You did say ... when we talked about it ...'

'You were so determined to fight me, weren't you?' he said tenderly. 'And because of that I responded as I

184

did. Do you still think I would force Amorel into a way of living in which she would be unhappy? Do you, my darling?'

She looked at him and then shook her head, impulsively catching his hand and cradling it to her face. 'Tell me about the house of the amulet, and the story of the amulet.'

He settled back, drawing her even closer and said slowly: 'It goes back to the time when my grandfather was a young man. He had quarrelled with his family, weary of the sterile provincial life which he felt was smothering him, and ran away when he was nineteen. He went first to Lebanon, drifted to Egypt, then Algiers, and finally to Morocco. He came to Kadir, then a tiny community, very poor, but with possibilities for a young man with vision. He began to plant, and soon prospered, but he shared his prosperity with those who worked for him and they came to love him. Then one day, when he was travelling far south on the fringe of the Sahara, he came upon a slave market. He was horrified, believing that French and English efforts were succeeding in eradicating this inhuman trade. But remember, this was more than sixty years ago, and even today slave trading still exists in isolated pockets in the Middle East,' he added grimly.

She shivered, and his arm tightened protectively as he went on: 'There was a young Berber girl, little more than a child, being led up on to the auction stage. She was trying desperately not to cry, and when the ghastly spiel started, the crude recital of her assets, my grandfather raged. He had a companion, a much older man, a hardened trader, who forcibly restrained him from attempting violent action. He suggested my grandfather should buy her if he felt so squeamish, never thinking my grandfather would take this suggestion seriously. But he did, and brought her back to Kadir, where he offered her her freedom and restored her to her people. By then he was enchanted by her, and a few months later he married her.'

Raoul paused, and the lights of reflection were grave in his eyes. 'It was the beginning of a long and most wonderful partnership. But it bore a shadow. His family severed all connection, refused to recognise his marriage or the three children born of it. My grandfather never returned to France and never saw his family again, but before he died he told me he had no regrets.'

'What was her name?' Melissa asked.

'Tamzen,' he responded, 'and now I must tell you a little of our family so that you will understand how these events in which you have been caught came about. My father was the eldest son, Martine was the only daughter—she was the mother of Amorel—and Jules was the younger son. He became curious as to the relatives in France whom he had never met. When he was sixteen he went to France for a holiday and sought the family, and there became influenced by them. From that day he changed. He never forgave my grandfather for giving him Berber blood and did everything possible to erase all traces of it in himself. He became wild and arrogant, and finally left Kadir for good. The girl he fell in love with refused to marry him, and eventually he married a young widow in Marseilles and settled down to take over the business her late husband had left. Soon he was bankrupt and was forced to turn to my grandfather for money.

Grandfather set him up again, and then a second time, against his better judgement and persuaded by Tamzen, the very object of Jules's hate, until at last my grandfather disowned him. When Tamzen died five years ago Jules came back and there was another bitter quarrel over money; it was then that my grandfather made the change in his will. He had intended that Kadir should be mine, because I would continue to administer it as he wished, and that his lifetime savings should be divided equally among his children and grandchildren. But bitterness had crept in. Martine, of course, was dead, and he saw no reason why those who had refused to share his home and adopted country should benefit.'

'And the amulet?' Melissa prompted softly.

'Grandfather had that made for Tamzen. She never lost her superstitious belief in such symbols, and when she was dying she insisted I have it. She brought me up,' he said quietly. 'She was the only mother I ever knew.'

Melissa stirred and took his hand, her caress of understanding instantly returned. A memory of something he had said the previous day came back to her and she said slowly:

'Last night, at the oasis, you spoke of history repeating itself and the story ap . . .' She stopped and looked down; she would not remind him of the way in which he had concluded the remark. 'Is this why you were so anxious that Amorel should return to Kadir and make it her home?'

'No, it has nothing to do with Amorel at all. It is to do with you.'

'Me? Oh, you mean . . .' her eyes widened and she

felt impatience at her slow comprehension, 'you mean because you had to rescue me, and now we . . .'

'And now we are what?' A teasing note belied the gravity of his expression and he tilted up her chin. 'You blush adorably, my darling. You have not yet got used to the idea of becoming the bride of Kadir?'

'I can't help blushing when you look at me like that,' she returned, regaining a little composure and even a desire to test his mettle to teasing. 'Are you glad now you rescued me and my donkey?'

'Hm, the animal may be useful, if it is not already so fat and lazy it will refuse to work at all.'

'Oh, Raoul,' she laughed happily, 'you have a sense of humour. That makes it perfect.'

He looked down at her radiant face and his own took on a seriousness. 'Am I perfect in your eyes, my little one?'

She gave a tiny inclination of her head, and then, because of her deeply generous heart and her flowering love, she cast off false pride and reached up to press her cheek against his. 'You are perfect now because I love you so very much.'

He held her close and she felt the sigh run through him as he whispered against her hair: 'I hope you will always feel that way, because I have not yet told you the rest of the story. My cousin told you of the garden, and the English bride who would not stay with her husband and child, but she could not tell you how that marriage followed the pattern which *Kismet* formed for the men of the Germont line. My father also met his bride in distressing circumstances. She was a young dancer, with a restless urge to travel the world. When my father met her she had come to Cairo with five other young English girls to dance in a night club cabaret. But they found that their contract committed them to other forms of entertaining beside dancing. Naturally they walked out, and then found that the agent who had fixed the engagement had been less than reputable and couldn't be contacted. The other girls had parents or relatives to help them out of their difficulties and get them home, but Jeanette was an orphan and found herself stranded and penniless, with the threat of the night club owner sueing her for breach of contract. It was then my father was able to help and get her clear. He also brought her home to Kadir, and married her, but unlike Tamzen she could not settle, and,' he shook his head, 'I think you know the rest.'

'So I am the third,' she said slowly, after a silence.

'And the wheel has come full circle. This is why I tried to scorn your sweet sincerity and believe it to be mere sentiment,' he said quietly. 'You captured my heart the first day I saw you, your eyes sparkling with your anger because a defenceless creature was being ill used, yet beneath your courage you were defenceless yourself. But I remembered my mother and the heartbreak she brought my father, and so I fought my feelings for you, until you were snatched away and I realised how deep were those feelings.'

She stirred, feeling the rhythm of his heart quickening beneath her cheek, and knew that *Kismet* had indeed woven her life strand inextricably with that of this strange, arrogant man of the desert. He had made her his prisoner and she no longer wanted ever to escape. Wordlessly she met his seeking lips, her own pulse rising in response to the urgency of his ardour, until a great sigh shuddered through him and he relinquished his fierce claim of her mouth.

'Now it is I who must submit,' he said huskily. 'Desire urges me to make you my own this very moment. To give, to take, to seal, with the desert our couch, the sun's caress our veil, and the wild winds to witness our vows. But my heart tells me that this is not the right way for our love. And so, my beloved little copper rose, I am going to take you home, to where the world will witness our vows and you will truly belong to me.'

He held out his hands and drew her to her feet, within the protective circle of his arms. She looked up at him, still with wonderment in her eyes as she beheld the face of love, and saw the sun-burnish touch his dark head with fire.

'The storm's over,' she said exultantly.

For a long moment he looked down at her before he echoed: 'Yes, the storm is over.'

She saw the calm gold of the desert stretching to meet the blue, and from out of the blue haze the words of the sand-diviner's prophecy whispered back. Darkness and fear had not come from the desert, but truly the desert had held her destiny, and the golden amulet at her throat was truly her talisman. It had brought her to safety from danger, and it had brought her to love.

She put her hand within Raoul's as they walked side by side into the sea of gold and now she possessed new understanding of the man who had first stormed then captured her heart. At last the picture in the sand was whole and clear.

Peace was in her heart and content in her spirit as

she looked into the future and said softly:

'*Look not back upon the sea of night as you step upon the sands of morning. Allah will be with you always.*'

'*And you will not step alone,*' said Raoul.

Have You Missed Any of These Harlequin Romances?